To Caroline ~

May Love Jean touch
Your heart as much
as she healed mine.

JEMiles

"Jackie"

Thank you for a wonderful
dinner! Please come
see me in Atlanta ~

Roseflower Creek

J. L. Miles

a novel

1st Edition

CUMBERLAND HOUSE
NASHVILLE, TENNESSEE

Published by
CUMBERLAND HOUSE PUBLISHING, INC.
431 Harding Industrial Drive
Nashville, TN 37211
www.CumberlandHouse.com

www.RoseflowerCreek.com
Email the author at JLMiles@RoseflowerCreek.com

Cover design by Unlikely Suburban Design

Library of Congress Cataloging-in-Publication Data

Miles, J. L. (Jacquelyn L.), 1947–
Roseflower Creek : a novel / J. L. Miles.
p. cm.
ISBN 1-58182-240-5 (alk. paper)
1. Problem families—Fiction. 2. Rural conditions—Fiction. 3. Abused children—Fiction. 4. Murder victims—Fiction. 5. Stepfathers—Fiction. 6. Georgia—Fiction. 7. Girls—Fiction. I. Title.
PS3613.I53 R6 2001
813'.6—dc21

2001042187

Printed in the United States of America
1 2 3 4 5 6 7—06 05 04 03 02 01

To my husband, R.W. M., who made it possible, who built the fort and keeps me safe. And to my parents, Cliff and Lois Lee, who were always there, even when I thought they weren't.

* * *

To my favorite sisters: Sandi, Barbara, Vicki, and Lori. And to my children, Brett and Shannon, my treasures—and James and Kelly, equally cherished, who've not made it home.

* * *

Most of all, to all of you out there who
break bones and bruise hearts—with love,
hope, and prayers . . . that you'll stop.

acknowledgments

This book could not have been written without help from above. With deep gratitude to God for planting the seeds . . . and to His angels for helping them grow.

* * *

Special thanks to Judy Iakovou, who taught me the elements of fiction, and to Harriette Austin for her diligent instruction in the art of suspense, and to her students for putting up with me. Much love and gratitude to each of you.

Also, to Ron Pitkin and his staff at Cumberland House (especially Lisa Taylor, Stacie Bauerle, Teresa Wright, and Julie Jayne), who loved Lori Jean and believed in her story—without whose faith, dedication, and hard work, these pages, as such, would not exist. My deepest appreciation and warmest regards always.

The river has my body, but heaven has my heart.

—Author unknown

Lori Jean

From my heart to yours, in memory of all
the little children whose bodies were broken,
but whose spirits rose above it to flower.

Roseflower Creek

prologue

The morning I died it rained. Poured down so hard it washed the blood off my face. I took off running and kept going 'til my legs give out and I dropped down in the tall grass by the creek. The ground was real soggy; my shoulders and feet sunk right in. I curled up on my side and rocked my tummy and sucked in that Georgia red clay 'til it clung like perfume that wouldn't let go. Mud cakes and dirt cookies, some I'd baked in the sun just yesterday, filled my nose. They danced all blurry above me, inviting me back to their world a' make-believe. That one mixed with laughter and pretend, sugared all nice with wishes and dreams. I reached out to grab 'em, to get back to that place where they was, but the pain held me tight in a blanket of barbed wire. And them cookies, they plumb disappeared.

My arm was busted. My spleen was teared. My 'testines was split and my windpipe—it was pretty much broken up, too. I didn't know most of those words, not then. I saw 'em in the paper the very next day. I stood over my mama and watched her cry on the newspaper the sheriff man brought to her cell. All I knew was it hurt, that day in the grass. It hurt so bad, it like ta' killed me. I prayed for it to end—I *did.* I sure enough did.

He come looking for me then, my stepdaddy, Ray. Called out to me, his voice filled with liquor.

"Lori Jean! You git back here! Ya' hear me?" he said. I heared him, but I didn't answer. It made him crazy in the head.

"Ya' hear me, girl? You ain't *had* a beatin' like I'm gonna give ya'," he said. 'Course, he was wrong. He just give me one.

He found me then; stumbled over me in the grass. He yanked me up by my hair, but I didn't move. Then he grabbed my arm, that broken one. It was twisted like a bent stick. He must not of seen it though, 'cause he didn't pay it no mind. But, not to worry. It didn't hurt no more. Nothing hurt—it was mighty peculiar. Truth be known, I felt pretty good right about then. Kind of floating on a cloud, I was.

"Why do ya' *do* this to me, huh?" he said. He was so mad. He tried to drag me back to the trailer where we lived. That's when he seen—I couldn't walk. I couldn't breathe. He sure changed his tune. He started crying and carrying on, shaking me all about.

"Lori Jean, honey, wake up! Wake up, honey!" he yelled.

Then he dropped on down to his knees; he was holding me so nice. He had his arms wrapped all around me and he was hugging me to his chest, just like a regular daddy, just like I always wanted him to. He was crying real tears. He was! And he was praying, too, right out loud.

"Oh Jesus!" he said, and he cried even harder. It was so sad.

"Oh my girl, my sweet baby girl," he said over and over. He was carrying on and hugging me so nice. I wanted to hug him right back, but my arms and legs—they wouldn't move nohow.

"What have I done to you, girl?" he asked, maybe thinking

I could answer. And then he started praying again and that was really something 'cause he never been one to pray much, even though my mama tried to get him to and drug him off ta' church ever' chance she got.

"Jesus, Mary, and Joseph, what have I done?" he said, and he picked me up.

I watched him carry me on down to Roseflower Creek and dump me in the water. So here I am, floating on a cloud, floating in the river, right in the middle of the creek! It's real pretty here. A body might could grow to like this even. Real peaceful like, it is. If'n my meemaw was here, she'd say, "This is plain out, plumb nice." And she'd be dead right. 'Cause that it is. That it sure enough is.

chapter one

My real daddy left in August when I was five on a day so hot they was giving out free fans. Drove away in our old pickup truck the color of money, which was *God-ronic* my meemaw said, since he ne'er had any. I don't remember much about my pa, but I remember that truck. He let me ride in the back whenever we drove to town. Like to throwed me out a couple a' times, but I loved it, being too little to realize a body could get killed that way. It was my favorite thing to do and the funnest, us not having much money for regular fun things.

"Headed to Atlanta," Daddy said that day. "Had enough a' yer' ma's bellyaching for sure."

She run after him, my ma did, her belly jiggling with a baby inside. Didn't do her no good. Daddy kept on going 'til he was a speck the size of the fleas that drove Digger nuts. Mama throwed herself off a ladder that night, from the hayloft in old man Hawkins's barn. She lived. Sprung her ankles is all. Both of 'em. But that baby, it died. It come out in the tub. That's when I seen it was a baby brother she had growing in there, 'cause I peeked.

Mama cried a long time, but not for the baby I don't think.

It was my daddy she wanted. She didn't mention that baby again, even when I growed older. Didn't name him or visit him like me and MeeMaw did. MeeMaw called him Paul after that guy in the Bible the preacher liked to talk about most Sundays. I called him Paulie. Seemed only right, him being so little. Truth be known, I'da rather had a sister. But a brother'd been okay.

The ladies at church said my daddy was no good; on a "slow train to hell," they said. I don't know; he was going real fast when he left. They said he had a girl over in Athens. 'Course that was a lie. I was his only girl. He told me so.

"You're my girl, Lori Jean," he said. "My only girl. And don't you forget it, okay?" he told me every time I sat in his lap.

'Course I never did understand him running off and leaving me with Mama. She didn't seem to want me much, either. 'Least she didn't throw me off no ladder. Poor Paulie. MeeMaw put him in a shoebox and tied it with the piece of blue satin ribbon she was saving for something special and this was something pretty special—a little dead baby boy never did no harm to no one and him being put in a shoebox and a mama that didn't cry over him or nothing.

The church folks let us bury him in a grave spot we didn't have no money for, which was real nice of them, so I forgive 'em right then for saying that stuff about my pa and that girl. We buried Paulie in the back, over by the kudzu. MeeMaw, that's what I call my grandma, and me would visit him on holidays and sometimes after Sunday service if the message moved her and her arthritis didn't hurt her too much to walk the extra steps.

Anyway, that was a long time ago. I'm ten now. I live with my mama and Ray. He's my stepdad. MeeMaw died two years back. That's when Ray moved in. MeeMaw didn't like for him to come round much when she was alive. Called him trailer trash. I wondered how that made him different; folks in town called me that when they didn't think I heard—but I did.

MeeMaw was right. Ray *was* trash. He was also the dog-gonist, meanest, orneriest, God-awful man I ever knowed in my whole ten years, the devil included. I dreamed *him* in a nightmare once, and he weren't nothing next to Ray. How my mama stood him, much less loved him, is beyond me.

MeeMaw told me she worshiped the ground Grandpa walked on. He died right after I was born. I figured Mama musta worshiped Ray like that, her bowing down to him. It was only later I seen it was fear. Fear that held her down, fear that paralyzed her, fear that let her let him kill me. Fear—it put her there in that jailhouse in Georgia; had her waiting on that 'lectric chair. Fear. Mz. Pence, my favoritist schoolhouse teacher, told me a famous president—Roozevelt, I think—said *all* we gotta fear is fear itself. He sure was right. I wonder how he knew. Maybe he had a mama had that kind a' fear. Maybe he had a mama waitin' on the hot seat somewhere. Maybe . . .

After Daddy left, nothing much happened 'til I was seven. He come back that summer for a spell. That was before Ray. They signed some papers, he and my mama. Then he left. He didn't mention me being his girl no more and I cried. MeeMaw told me not to mind. Said I had a daddy in heaven who'd watch over me always and not to worry, he'd never leave me; that he was holding me in his arms, keeping me safe that very moment. I asked him to please, if 'n he could, to hold me a bit tighter—I couldn't feel a thing.

That summer Digger run off. He done that once before we knowed of. He run off from wherever he used to live. That's how we ended up having him as our dog. MeeMaw said

Digger was like some kind of men.

"What kind is that?" I asked.

"The kind you can't count on," she said.

That was the summer Melvin and Lexie come ta' stay with us for a spell. I see now that was the beginning of the end. Yep, sure enough. That's what it was, all right—the beginning of the end.

chapter two

Looking back, I 'spect things woulda been a whole lot different if Lexie had never married Melvin and brought him around that summer. I probably might still be alive even. Lexie was my ma's best friend when they was growing up, like Carolee is mine.

Lexie was the most beautiful woman I ever seen, not counting picture magazines. Looked just like a movie star even; exceptin' her hair. It weren't any color I ever seen on a movie star 'less you count Howdy Doody. But that was before she went to the Cut 'n' Style and had it done right. Then it looked a whole lot better; sort of a cross between Howdy Doody and Rhonda Fleming. Wanda Puckett—she owns the beauty shop—she fixed it up for her. Wanda's real good with hair, but MeeMaw said she smacked her gum too loud, like ta' drove her nuts and she quit going.

"It's the best I can do, sweetie," Wanda told Lexie. She didn't use her scissors much that day. Even so, Lexie's hair got shorter. Some of the ends just broke off in Wanda's hands. Lexie cried and cried, which hurt my heart 'cause I loved her already and wished she was my ma and sometimes pretended she was.

"Lexie Ann, stop that sniffling," Wanda said. "After what you dumped on your head, girl, you best be thankful for what hair you got left."

"I ain't gonna be thankful for *that,* Wanda!" Lexie said. "That's like bein' glad your house burned down and only took out half your kids."

"Well ain't you the dramatic one now," Wanda said. "And ungrateful, too. You best bite your tongue, Lexie, 'fore the good Lord puts it in mind to befall sorrow on the rest a' this here mess." Wanda run her styling comb through Lexie's hair and sure enough, plenty more strands fell out.

"See?" she said.

Lexie started crying again and dabbed at her eyes. I hugged her lap and told her she looked better'n anyone I ever seen with their hair half gone, even though Homer Bailey, the goat man, was the only one I knowed like that. From then on, Lexie always let Wanda do her hair real regular. And she'd take me with her, too. I remember one time we was just talking and laughing, having us a fine old time doing nothing.

"Lori Jean, honey," she said, "I do believe it's time we head to the beauty shop. What'cha think, baby girl?" she asked and waited for my answer just like I was a grownup and counted.

She was putting on lipstick and fussing in the mirror at the dressing table Melvin fixed for her. It was the mirror her mama give her 'fore she died, so it was real special, for sure. It was the kind of mirror you don't even have to hang on to. It stood up in place all by itself. It sat on a long, pretty scarf Lexie draped over a board resting on two peach crates Melvin hauled in for her. MeeMaw sewed a right pretty skirt for it even. Real nice, just like the kind the ladies in the movies have. Lexie was a whole lot like the ladies in the movies. She even walked like that Marilyn one the men all whistle at, only Lexie did it better. She didn't act stupid or nothing when she did it. She just talked normal like and smiled and walked along with her sides moving that way all on their own. I tried it myself and it didn't work, so I knowed it just come natural to her. Me and Marilyn had to work at ours and it showed.

I practiced walking like Lexie every night 'fore prayers, before MeeMaw come to tuck me down. I figured I had a lot of time to get it right, which was good 'cause mine resembled Myrtle Soseby's, the church lady. She had one leg shorter than the other and walked with a wiggle, too—only no men whistled.

"Melvin, honey," Lexie said that day, "give me some money, sugar. We girls need to git ourselves all gussied up for the weekend." She walked that wiggly walk on over to Melvin and sat right down in his lap. He sniffed her hair real good and smacked his lips and said he was gonna gobble her up. He's so funny. He was always saying things like that. Lexie loved Melvin and I did, too. He was a big old teddy bear, he was, with a Santa belly. It hung over his belt buckle whenever he stood up and jiggled when he walked.

It was hard for me to understand my stepdaddy Ray being his brother, same ma and pa even. Didn't make no sense a'tall. They was nothing alike. Didn't even look alike. Carolee told me where babies come from and how they was made after Connie Dee, her older sister, told her. So I figured Melvin and Ray's ma had a different daddy helping her make one of them and their pa just never knew, 'cause how'd he know 'less she told him and that didn't sound like something a ma'd tell a pa, 'less she weren't right in the head or wanted a good whupping.

One time Ray punched my mama's eyes and her nose real good for just looking back at a fella that looked at her first. They swelled all up and turned black and she stayed in the house 'til they turned yellow and purple. Then she come out again. Lexie helped her put makeup on 'em and we all went to church that Sunday, even Ray. Her eyes stayed funny for a while, then they got better, but her nose never did look like mine again.

Ray said she had a big mouth and he'd redesign her lips, too, if she didn't learn to shut it. But she didn't and her mouth got cut up bad a couple of times. It wan't 'til she got it all stitched up that she stopped talking back to him. By then she didn't much look like the same mama no more. Her nose had a hump in it and when she smiled, which weren't often, her front tooth was missing. Ray said we didn't have no money to git her a new one, but I saved any money I got, mostly pennies, just in case I could get enough put up for Christmas. How much could one little old tooth cost anyway?

But I reckon she should of shut up while she still had her pretty face or kicked him out 'fore he wrecked it. For sure she'd have her front tooth, and she probably wouldn't have to be in that jail, going to that courthouse with those chains on her ankles that they roped up to her waist. I probably might still be there, too—with Carolee, down at the creek, swinging on that rope, just running and playing, making up a batch of them mud cookies. But knowing Ray, I guess he wouldn't of stayed kicked out anyway. He was as big as he was mean. He did what he wanted. Somebody bigger and stronger than my mama would of had to stop him.

I prayed Melvin would, but he didn't. Guess he couldn't, Ray being the older brother and all, out a' respect or something.

Then they got their own place. He and Lexie. By the time Ray started in on me, they weren't around to see it. I wondered if Melvin would of stopped him then. Mostly I wondered if Lexie would of *made* Melvin stop him. I thought about it every time Ray got hold of me. I cried about it when he busted my eardrum and it hurt so bad and Mama poured warm oil in it and pushed a plug of cotton in to keep it there. I hated the feeling of that stuff as it trickled into my head. Mama said to stay out of his way and to run and hide when he got the liquor out, which didn't make no sense. I'da been hiding all the time I wasn't in school 'cause he got hisself fired and weren't working no more.

Most of that bad stuff didn't start 'til after MeeMaw died. She got the flu, the kind that come all the way from China. I was eight. She died in her sleep out on the porch. 'Neumonia. I hated that porch from then on. It weren't nothing but a mud room leading to the back step, anyway, but it was her spot and she wouldn't hear of giving it up. I knew it was too cold out there. Mama knew, too, and fussed at her all the time about it. That was one thing about my ma. She loved MeeMaw as much as I did. She loved MeeMaw the way I wanted her to love me.

Melvin and Lexie coming was about the best thing that ever happened to me and the worst thing, too. Carolee said that was a paradox. She's real smart. Read it to me right out of a book, *It was the best of times; it was the worst of times.*

Melvin, he was looking for work at the Scottsdale Cotton Mill clear over in Decatur. Heard they was hiring and drove over from Birmingham after Lexie's mama died. He found work straightaway and they found a temporary place to stay with us, MeeMaw saying it was our Christian duty to look out for those that needed a helping hand.

Things was about perfect, too, 'til Ray got word the mill was hiring and he showed up. Mama fell for him right off. The first thing I noticed 'bout Ray was he picked his nose and had bad breath. Mama must not of cared, her being so lonely. Ray didn't cotton to church none, talked hisself a filthy mouth

MeeMaw said, and she run him off. Told Melvin right out how it was.

"You and Lexie is welcome to stay a piece, 'til you git settled," she said, "but that no-count brother a' yours is not welcome to put another foot on my doorstep."

"Yes, ma'am," Melvin said. He was real respectful to my meemaw, he was.

"He's a lost soul, that one, ma'am," Melvin said, and he shook his head from side to side real sad like.

"Amen," MeeMaw whispered back, and she nodded her head real sad like, too.

"Reckon we should pray for him right now, ma'am?"

"Glory be," MeeMaw answered.

And Melvin, he led us in prayer. MeeMaw bowed her head and closed her eyes. Melvin winked at me and Lexie and then he said a prayer as good as any preacher.

MeeMaw liked Melvin. She liked Lexie all right, too, I guess, but prayed real funny when Lexie was around.

"Sweet, merciful Jesus," she said once when Lexie was all fixed up nice for church. And another time, Lexie wore the prettiest yellow sundress that scooped down in the front and jiggled when she moved and MeeMaw said, "Mercy! Lord a' mercy!" She shook her head and looked up at the ceiling like it was heaven itself.

"God help us all," she said. Stuff like that. We was only going to a picnic and I thought Lexie looked real nice. All the men did, too. She was the center of attention that day. Just beautiful. They musta couldn't believe how good that yellow dress went with her red hair 'cause their eyes followed her wherever she went that day, 'til they drunk too much whiskey and couldn't follow their own feet and some of them fell down even. MeeMaw prayed for them, too.

Lexie had a special way with people, 'specially men and most 'specially Melvin.

"Melvin, honey, reach on down in yore pocket, sugar, and give your sweetie all you got," she said, and he did. He give her all the money he dug out of his jeans.

"Gosh, is he always this nice?" I asked.

"Pretty much."

"And you always get what you want?" I said, not understanding. Mama never got nothing from Ray but trouble.

"Uh-huh," she said and smiled this itsy-bitsy smile where just the corners of her mouth turned up and her eyes twinkled like Christmas.

"How come?"

"It's a secret, sugar."

"Oh, tell me, please, please!" I begged, thinking I could pass it on to my mama so's Ray'd be nice to her, too.

"Well, sweetie, I get what I want," she said and turned and whispered in my good ear, " 'cause I got what he wants."

"Oh . . . ," I said nice like, but I was plumb disappointed. Mama didn't much have what Ray wanted, I guess. He just wanted that bottle and he wanted those young girls he met down at the tavern. I heard her yell that at him one morning when they was fighting over where he'd been all night.

"Go on now, " Lexie said. "Fix yourself up real pretty, baby girl. We're going shoppin', too." Lexie was getting herself a set and style most every week now. One time she even got herself one a' them permanent waves, which stunk real bad at first. Before shopping we headed to the Cut 'n' Style. Lexie picked out a different color for Wanda to use on her hair. Wanda had these little ponytails for Lexie to pick from, looked like they come off the back end of itty-bitty horses. She pointed to one with some gold in it.

"See, honey, in't it pretty?" she asked me.

"Uh-huh."

"Now, don't be tellin' peoples I dye my hair, Lori Jean, hear?" she said. "There's a few things a proper girl keeps to herself. Her hair color and her bust size is two of 'em."

That sounded reasonable to me and I decided I'd keep those things to myself for sure. It weren't hard since I wasn't planning on changing the color of my hair. It was near black and Carolee said it was hair sent by the angels. Hers was blonde. And keeping my bust size secret weren't no problem, neither, being I didn't have none yet. But I decided when I got me some, I wouldn't tell anyone what size they was 'cause I wanted to be just like Lexie, excepting for my hair. I couldn't see changing it, mine being sent from the angels themselves and all.

Lexie tried on dress after dress that day. She settled on a pink sundress with little baby straps and she bought me one, too. She did! She honest to golly did. I liked to 'bout died of excitement right on the spot. It was white with a crocheted collar. It had these tiny flowers peppered all over it with lace all around the hem. Said I looked like a princess. I don't know about that, but I sure felt like one. I never wanted to take it off. I woulda slept in that dress, but I was afraid I'd get it all wrinkled and ruin it 'fore Sunday. After church the next day we went to the fair. MeeMaw made Lexie put a sweater on over her shoulders 'cause of the straps on her dress being thin as spaghetti.

"Missy," she said, "I got enough faith to move mountains, so I don't have enough left to count on those straps holdin' up melons the size a' Georgia!"

"Oh my, my," Lexie said. She acted real surprised to hear words like that come out of MeeMaw. I weren't too surprised. MeeMaw had more'n one side to her. I heard her curse once even, when Maybelle Hawkins's grandson stole Rosie, her roosting hen.

"Lewis Hawkins, you run off with my hen!"

"Did not."

"You did!"

"No ma'am."

"You little shit! I seen you with my own two eyes," she said and chased him clear down the road, dust flying in all directions. Caught him, too. About wrung his neck the way he must of wrung Rosie's. He and Chester Britt roasted that chicken over a fire down by the creek and ate it. I saw 'em. I never did tell, though, it being her favorite hen and all.

MeeMaw was plumb full of wisdom. She had a lot of 'pinions, too, and she passed them on whenever they come to her.

"Missy, the Lord didn't put those bosoms there to test the strong and tempt the weak," she said to Lexie one morning 'fore we left for church.

"'Course he didn't," Lexie said.

"Then tuck 'em back in 'fore some fool grabs 'em!" MeeMaw said. Lexie did like she was told, no questions asked.

After church, at the fair, we run into Maybelle Hawkins.

"Lexie Ann!" Maybelle run over to hug her. "Why it's been ten years if it's been a day!"

Lexie hugged her back, but she didn't look none too happy to see her. I could tell.

"You sweet thang. Don't you look good, now," Maybelle said.

She kind a' looked like a hawk 'cause of her nose. And she had a real fat body with funny little bird legs, too. I felt sorry for her and hoped people wouldn't laugh 'cause that'd be real mean, but truth be known, I was having trouble not laughing at her a little myself.

"How long's it been—how old are you now?" Maybelle asked. Her voice was big as she was and she talked real loud.

Lexie said it certainly had been a long time and it'd be nice to chat, but we had to get going.

"Lori Jean hasn't even rode the merry-go-round yet and here we got us two tickets left," Lexie said and grabbed my arm.

I thought we'd used the last ones on the funhouse, which weren't even much fun, so I was real happy finding out we had us two more, but in truth we didn't.

"Lori Jean, when you're grown," Lexie told me when we left, "don't *ever* tell your age! A woman who'll tell her age will tell *anything*.

"Another thing, stay clear a' that woman. Maybelle Hawkins will do you more harm than a hurricane that hits in the night—and don't you forget it."

Turned out she was right. But I did forget. On my tenth birthday, I shared a secret with Maybelle after she coaxed me. When she called the law, I remembered what Lexie said. By then it was too late. That's when all our lives changed—and I don't mean for the better.

chapter three

When a girl got a daddy who's run off and a mama beat up and hurtin', there ain't a lot of happy times, but the summer Lexie Ann found out she and Melvin was having a baby sure was one of them. She went to this doctor and he give her this test with a rabbit and it showed she was having a baby for sure. She was real glad. Only thing, that poor little rabbit, it died. That was real sad.

"See, honey, if the rabbit lives, that means I'm not pregnant. So don't you be sad now, hear?" Lexie told me. "They got a whole bunch of rabbits, sugar. They's just doin' their part is all, okay?"

I told her it was, but it really wasn't. After that, every time I seen a lady fixing to have a baby, I thought about those little rabbits. Maybe they was doing their part and all, but who asked 'em if they wanted to anyway? Seems like them smart doctors could come up with a better way to tell someone they was having a baby than killing a cute little rabbit, hopping around, minding his own business.

I decided I wasn't ever having me a baby 'til they found another way. I wasn't in any hurry to make one when I growed up anyway. That day Carolee told me how a lady and a man made one, it didn't sound like much fun to me nohow. Carolee said it was. Said her sister Connie Dee did it with her boyfriend in the hayloft on Friday night when their ma and pa was at the church revival. They caught her watching and give her a quarter to hush up. And Carolee said her cousin Millie Anne done it once, too, with a fella never called her again and she liked it real fine. Still, I don't know . . . seemed right peculiar to me, girl parts and boy parts plumb joined up. I sure couldn't imagine Melvin and Lexie doing something like that. Still, they was having a baby—but what other choice did they have anyway? They probably wanted one so bad they done what they had to, then just put it out of their minds. I'm pretty sure of that 'cause they's real nice folks, they is, go to church regular like and everything, they sure do.

When we got back from the doctor's, Lexie told Melvin straightaway about the baby.

"Heeeeeehaaaaa!" Melvin was dancing Lexie all around in a circle, 'til she got herself all dizzy.

"Melvin, I'm gonna have this baby six months sooner than it's time if you don't stop that!" Lexie said and she sunk right down against him.

"Oh, baby girl, baby girl," he said to me. "We're gonna have ourselves a little baby. What'd you think about that?"

"Oh, that's about the next best thing to Christmas, I reckon," I said. "Better even."

Mama come in the room and sat down on the sofa. She looked kinda poorly. Her eye was swollen on one side. She had her hair hung over the front of it, but I could still tell. That's what she always done when she was trying to hide it. She weren't eating much again, so she was real thin and she was a pretty thin mama to start with, so that weren't good.

Ray, he was staying out all night. Twice this week I knowed of, so they was fussing at each other. I sure hoped she'd leave him be 'fore he hurt her again real bad. Why'd she care if he stayed out all night anyway? I was hoping he'd stay out all year. Suit me fine.

"Mama, Lexie's havin' herself a baby. Now ain't that nice?" I asked her.

"Babies cost money—that part ain't nice. The rest's okay, I guess," she said.

Mama looked so sad I run over to give her a hug. I sat down next to her and just patted her shoulder.

"Don't be sad, Mama. We're gonna have a little baby round here to love."

"Babies is real sweet," she said.

"MeeMaw always said babies is gifts from the angels, 'member?" I told her and just kept patting her, wanting her to be happy like us, about anything even. Just happy.

"Yes, babies is real sweet," Mama said, and she patted me back. Then she leaned over and kissed me on the cheek. "And you're real sweet, too, Lori Jean." It was the nicest thing my mama ever said to me. After that, whenever I'd get sad, I'd think to when Mama told me that and 'fore long I'd forget all about being sorrowful.

* * *

Come winter, MeeMaw wasn't around to sew some pretty clothes for Lexie to wear. Her belly was getting bigger every week now. So she bought herself some fabric and a dress pattern, and we hauled out MeeMaw's old sewing machine and got to work.

"Baby girl, I'm gonna lay out this here material on the floor, see?" Lexie said. "Then I want you to pin the pattern pieces here to the fabric for me, okay?"

Lexie couldn't bend over hardly a'tall, so I pinned them pieces down the way I remembered MeeMaw doing it. We was making a dress with long sleeves and a bow in front, kinda like a sailor dress or something.

"Okay, sugar, now just cut all around them pieces," Lexie said, and handed me MeeMaw's pinking shears. They was real peculiar-looking, like regular scissors 'cept they had these jagged teeth all around the edges.

"These pieces sure enough don't look like anything that would fit a body part, Lexie," I said.

"Well, honey, that's 'cause we gotta fold them over and sew 'em together. Then it's gonna look like this, see?" She held up the front of the envelope the pattern come in. A lady with yellow hair was wearing the dress, showing how it would look, only hers was dark brown. Ours was red-and-navy plaid with some green and black in it. We bought that 'cause it was on sale. Fifty-nine cents a yard and the lady at the sewing place said it was a real bargain. Only we forgot to tell her we was beginners. Maybe then she would of told us it wan't such a bargain.

Lexie sewed all the pieces together. She was real excited and I was kinda, but not too much 'cause I thought it still looked funny, but I didn't want Lexie to know that 'cause she worked so hard on it. When she got it finished, she tried it on.

"How's it look?" she asked me.

"Um, it looks, um, it looks nice, I think," I said, but I was telling a big ol' lie. Truth be known, it looked mighty peculiar. The plaid lines in the fabric was going every which way. It plumb changed direction every time it run into a different seam. Made my eyes go crossed just lookin' at it.

"Do I look okay?" Lexie asked.

"Well . . ." I was trying to say something good about it when Melvin come in. Lexie turned to him right off.

"Melvin, honey, what do you think a' my dress? All I gotta do is hem up the bottom." Lexie swirled around so he could get a good look.

"Honey, that dress belongs on a kilt somewhere in Scotland. Where'd you get that crazy thing?" Melvin said.

Lexie started crying right off. She was doing a lot of that lately. Her hormone things was goin' haywire, Mama said. She said it happened to her, too, when I was growing in her belly.

"Melvin, I *made* this dress, myself! Lori Jean and me, we been here for hours workin' on it."

"I'm sorry, sugarplum," Melvin said. "Maybe I just didn't see it in the right light." Melvin guided Lexie by the shoulders over to the window.

"You just stand right there. Let me take a second look," he said.

"Okay, what do you think?" Lexie asked. "Now, don't be tellin' me no lies, Melvin Pruitt."

"Well, honey, in that case, I think we oughta go get you one them store-bought maternity dresses. That darn thing looks like the dickens."

"Oh, Melvin!" Lexie wailed, and she run off crying with Melvin running after her.

"Now, honey . . . ," he said. "You said you wanted me to tell you the . . ."

I didn't much hear the rest. I decided it was as good a time as any to head back home. I coulda told Melvin a woman might ask for the truth, but mostly she don't wanna hear it. 'Leastin' that's what MeeMaw always said.

I left them to work it out and went on over to Carolee's to

see if her mama would let her go down to the creek for a spell. We met at school in second grade, when her daddy come here looking for work. Times was hard. Lots of folks come here looking for work in the mills. We had a passel of cotton mills round these parts, carpet mills, too.

Carolee and me got to be friends right off. She come in the middle of the school year. Our class didn't have an extra desk for her at first, so Mz. Pence give her a chair to pull up next to mine so's she could share my desktop 'til they found her one.

Carolee wasn't stuck on herself like some girls in the class. She didn't boast none, neither. And she didn't insist on always having her way. It was my lucky day when she come to our school. Carolee was the kind a' friend a body'd be lucky to get once in a lifetime. And here I got one. Fancy that!

Carolee sure was pretty and a whole lot a' fun, too. Me and her used to meet up before school and walk the rest of the way together. She had herself a umbrella, too, and when it rained she shared it with me 'cause I didn't have one. That way I only got rained on part of the way. And when it rained real hard, Carolee left early and come all the way to my house to get me, just so I wouldn't get so wet running up to meet her. That's how special a friend she was 'cause coming to get me was clear out of her way.

We used to spend most our time down at Roseflower Creek. Before MeeMaw died she told me the story of how it got called that. It was a real nice story. Folks said it was pretty much true. A long time 'fore any of 'em was born, there was a woman who come by all the small towns in these parts and sold wildflowers to make her living.

"She didn't have no family to look after, Lori Jean," MeeMaw explained. "She made the countryside her family and visited every nook and valley as the months wore on, selling her flower seeds along the way."

"What happened to her, MeeMaw?"

"Well no one likely knows for sure, child, but from what we can put together, she left one morning and headed to the creek yonder and nobody ever seen her again."

"Nobody a'tall?"

"Not a one."

"What do *you* figure happened to her, MeeMaw?" I asked. It seemed to me a body come visiting what they took to be their family just wouldn't stop without so much as a 'howdy do.'

"Well I'll tell ya'," MeeMaw said, "that creek she headed to—that one you and Carolee spend so much time at—it had those chinaberry trees and the longleaf pines that's so pretty that rest along its banks. And it had the handful a' red maples that's still there. It had all that moss running down towards the water, covering dead branches along the way. But it didn't have no flowers."

MeeMaw was working on another quilt and her fingers was busy stitching a bright red square of cotton onto a patch of pale blue silk. She wasn't giving this one to the church bazaar, though. She was making it for my very own bed. Come winter I was gonna be warm as butter melting on toast.

"That spring after no one sees her again, flowers was blooming everywhere along that creek, Lori Jean."

"Gosh. Just like that?" I said.

"Just like that. Folks called 'em Rose's flowers. That was her name. Rose. Said she musta grown tired a' all her travels and just lay down there and passed on, real peaceful like."

MeeMaw took her glasses off and rubbed at the corners of her eyes.

"The older I get, child, the more spots I see," she said. She always said that after long hours of quilting. She blinked and put her glasses back on real careful like.

"After a while as more and more folks moved here, they drew up a town charter, called it Millwood. Everything they planted grew in abundance. Cotton, corn, soybeans. Folks said it was because her spirit resided down at Rose's flower creek and watched over them and their crops. They thanked God for Rose's creek and for all their blessings they thought it brung 'em. 'Fore long lazy tongues turned Rose's flower creek to Roseflower Creek. It caught on and here we are."

"That's a real nice story, MeeMaw," I said.

"It's more than a story, Lori Jean. It's your heritage."

"What's a heritage?"

"Why, that's something that comes to you—that belongs to you by way a' your birth."

"You mean Roseflower Creek belongs to me?"

"It belongs to ever' one of us, child; ever' one of us who lives here. Mostly, we belong to it."

"All of us?"

"Yep. All of us," she said. "'Leastin' all of us who'll die here."

I told Carolee that story first chance I got, Roseflower Creek being our favorite spot and all. The water there ran all lazy like most the time. It had some fish we tried to catch with our hands, too, but we never got any. The flowers growing there were wild and near tall as us. We flattened out a spot between 'em to serve the mud cakes we made at the edge of the creek where the clay was all squishy. We mixed that clay with dirt we dug from the shallow water and had a fine old time making a mess of ourselves and our clothes.

Carolee's daddy ended up working at the Scottsdale Cotton Mill just like Ray, only he got hisself promoted to being first man right under the boss man. He told me I could come over to see Carolee whenever it suited me. He was real nice—funny, too.

"Lori Jean, you're welcome to come by anytime," he said. "Now we don't have nothin' fancy here. Ain't got a pot to pee in."

But he was just funnin'. They had themselves a pot inside that flushed even. They was real lucky. We still used the shed out back. A couple of times Ray covered it over, dug another hole and moved it to another spot. Mostly he drunk too much, so it didn't get moved regular and it stunk something awful when the wind blowed.

Carolee's daddy did some farming on the side, like a lot of folks did to grow some a' their own food. Not too long after Carolee's daddy started working at the cotton mill, he hired Ray to fix his tractor when it broke down. I didn't know Ray could do anything like that. Turns out he really couldn't. He just said he could 'cause he wanted the money. He mostly used whatever extra money he got for liquor, so it never did us much good.

That was a real sad lie he told Carolee's pa, that he knowed about fixing tractors 'cause that one lie led to a whole chain a' lies. It's even sadder where we all ended up because of it. MeeMaw called it fate. She said life was one link looped to another like a fine-knitted sweater.

"Drop one stitch, child, and the rest unravels."

She sure was right. Ray dropped more than one stitch, and a lot of lives unraveled.

chapter four

MeeMaw always said if you hate something long enough, it'll come back and bite ya'. So I know it was real bad of me to hate Darla Faye Brewster like I did. I was asking for it for sure, but I just couldn't help myself. Darla's daddy was the foreman at the Scottsdale Cotton Mill. Chester Britt was her brother, only they had different last names 'cause they had different daddies. Chester's daddy run off like mine did when he was little, and later on his mama married Noble Brewster and they had Darla.

Nobody had much money around our parts. Most folks was 'bout as poor as the ones come before 'em. But Noble Brewster, he weren't as poor as the rest of us, him being the boss man at the mill and all. Darla Faye even had a shiny new red bicycle she got for Christmas one year. And when she banged it all up, well her daddy just got her another one.

That weren't why I hated her, though. I thought it was real nice of her daddy when he give her that bike. She looked real fine riding it to school, I even told her so. But all she did was stick out her tongue like I said something awful to her. Fancy that. I was trying to be nice and let her know I didn't hold no grudge against her for what she done to me when I was just a little kid starting out in school.

We was in first grade together, see. I wasn't real happy about going. I didn't have me any of that confidence, yet. I got me some when I met Carolee and then I got some more when I met Lexie, but that was later. So when I first started school I was real scared. I cried something awful to MeeMaw to let me back in the house 'cause Mama pushed me out on the back porch and locked the door.

"Go on now, Lori Jean," she said. "You gotta go to school. That's the law." I was six. I sure didn't understand anyone making a law to scare the daylights out of little kids. I stayed on that porch, crying and crying. Mama come out once to tell me I'd be late.

"Lori Jean, you get goin'. You'll be late your first day. They got a punishment for that!" she said.

I reckon she thought that might help me get moving. She weren't a mean mama or nothing. But all that did was send the terror that was stuck in my throat clear down to my stomach, where it all come up along with the grits I had for breakfast.

MeeMaw come outside then. She cleaned me up with a washcloth.

"Lori Jean, honey," she said. "All you gotta do is follow them rules the teacher sets out and you'll do just fine." I trusted MeeMaw. She never told me any lies before, so I couldn't see no reason for her starting in just then. I went down that long dirt road and made my way to school.

That year we had first, second, and third graders in our class all in one room. Mz. Pence was our teacher. She was real nice. I liked her right off. If I'da known she'd be so nice I might not of been scared a'tall. I might not of throwed my breakfast up even.

Things was looking pretty good that first week. We got sectioned off into reading groups; those that could and those that couldn't. 'Course I couldn't, not having been to school a'fore. I was a Yellowbird. There was another group of birds that couldn't read, neither. They was Robins. The rest, they was Bluebirds. They were the big kids. They'd already been to school for a long time a'fore us. They bossed us around when Mz. Pence wasn't looking.

Truth is, they strutted around like they was somebody and we weren't nobody. And we hadn't harmed anybody and was trying to please everybody. Add to that, we was fixin' to learn those letters that make up them words on the board we couldn't read. It was real hard. It was about all a body could stand.

Even so, things was going along pretty good. I remembered what MeeMaw told me about them rules. And I was following them and following them. It was the third or fourth day, I think.

Then Darla Faye ruined everything. Well, actually it was my own fault, but she didn't have to get her nose in edgewise. She made it a worse disaster than it already was. What happened is, one morning Mz. Pence, she had one of them reading groups, the Robins I think, up at the front in a circle reading about Spot jumping and Dick running and Jane seeing, stuff like that. Anyway, we wasn't to interrupt her 'lessen we had permission. Well, I had to go. So I was waving my hand and waving my hand to get me that permission. She didn't see me none. Then I *really* had to go, so I was praying and waving my hand and that didn't do no good, neither.

Now I weren't stupid, and I knew I should just up and leave right then and there, do my business and be done with it. But it was the strangest thing. I was scared to break the rules and my feet was stuck to the floor like they was plumb glued down. It was real sorrowful, 'cause I couldn't hold it no longer and it come trickling down my leg. 'Fore long it was running down both legs. It made a puddle right on the floor in front of God and everyone He made that was in that schoolroom.

If that weren't bad enough, that blabbermouth Darla Faye jumped right up and yelled out to everybody had ears. "Mz. Pence! *Lori Jean wet her pants! Lori Jean wet her pants!*" She yelled it out singsong like it were a tune on the hit parade. I wanted to kill that girl right on the spot and here I was a Christian even. My face was all hot. My shoes was all wet. They was squishing against my toes. I felt right poorly, I did.

And all them kids all around the room started clucking about like they was a group a' chickens fixing to get fed, and that Darla Faye was the lead hen. She got everybody pointing and laughing, making terrible fun of me. I tried hard not to cry, but I did anyway. I wanted that floor to open right up and swallow me down; sink me clear to China, I was hurting that bad inside.

Mz. Pence made it through all them hovering about me and shooed every one of them back to their desks.

"That's enough," she said. "Ya'll go on back to your desks right now and work your assignments."

She took my hand and we went out to the cloakroom. She knelt down on the wooden planks and took out her hanky. It was real pretty. It was white with lace on the ends and it had a pink rose on it with tiny little stitches. She dabbed at my tears, but they kept coming.

"Ssssshhhh," she said. "Don't cry, Lori Jean. Don't cry, honey. It's gonna be okay. I promise," she said.

She put the hanky up to my nose and waited for me to blow. I could smell the flowers in it. They smelled just like her. They smelled real good.

"There," she said. "That's better."

Then she folded that pretty hanky up and put it in my pocket. She did! And she said, "It's a very special hanky, Lori Jean, for a very special girl." Then she patted that hanky down in place. That was really something. She coulda took it home and washed it up good as new and here she give it to me.

She tilted my chin up high right next to hers.

"Go on home now, Lori Jean," she said. "Come back tomorrow—and don't be late," she told me. Her voice was as soft as the scarves MeeMaw knit.

"Tomorrow it'll be okay. You'll see," she said. "I promise."

My sweater was on the metal hook, lined up in a row with all the others. She knew which one was mine—she about knew everything. She took it down and helped me put it on. She even ignored the missing buttons and just patted the spots where they shoulda been.

Then she led me to the front door of that schoolhouse and sent me on my way. She waved, so I waved back. She smiled. I tried to. Then she nodded her head, but I didn't nod mine. I wan't real sure about tomorrow. But then her eyes just grabbed my eyes and hung on. It was so strange. I could see those words she said.

"It'll be okay—you'll see—you'll see." Her eyes was talking at me! And, don't you just know, it was. I loved Mz. Pence. I still do.

But that Darla Faye—if I was anything close to being alive, I'd probably still hate her. Which reminds me of another mean thing she done. This time to Carolee back before MeeMaw died. Makes me roast just thinking 'bout it.

chapter five

"I reckon I best wear that dress Lexie got me, MeeMaw. It's gonna be a real fancy party. Carolee's mama sewed a new dress for her, even, in that taffeta material's so pretty."

"Oh my," MeeMaw said.

"It's all white. And it's got pearl buttons; three of 'em right under the collar."

"Sounds right fancy, indeed," MeeMaw said. "You best let me do your hair, child. New hairdo might make your dress look brand-new."

"Her mama bought decorations, too."

"My, my," MeeMaw said.

Carolee was fixing to be eight, like me. My birthday come in April, only I didn't get me a party. Mama said, "Maybe next year, honey, we'll have us some extra money." So, I planned on having one myself that next year, maybe.

On the morning of Carolee's party, MeeMaw went ahead and fixed my hair real nice. She put some braids in it and tied it up on top with a ribbon even. Looked real pretty with my dress, the white one with the little roses and the lace all around. I'd weared it a lot already, but it was the only one I had that wasn't mended. I didn't much mind wearing it again. Carolee liked it real fine. She was always admiring it.

Carolee had invited all the kids our age from school. She didn't really want to invite that Darla, but what with Darla's daddy being the boss man and Carolee's daddy working for him there at the cotton mill, her ma said she had to. There was no getting around it.

"Don't you fret now, Carolee. You be gracious to her, hear?" her ma said. I told her not to fret none, either.

"Darla's mama always sends a good present along with her, Carolee. Just think about that, okay?" I told her.

"Trudy Anne got a tea set from her last year even. It was real pretty. I'd like to have me one a' them. We could take it down to the creek when we make them mud cookies. Wouldn't that be nice?" I asked her.

"It'd be nicer if she croaked," Carolee told me back. "We can play mud cookies without her dumb old tea set just fine."

Poor Carolee. It was her birthday and here she was sad over that Darla Faye already and she hadn't even showed up yet. I come early and helped put the party stuff out. Carolee's ma had little hats for us to wear and these noisemakers left over from New Year's evening night, but they was right nice for regular parties, too. Horns and rattlers and these funny things that whip out like a long curly tongue when you blow.

"I like these best, Carolee," I said. "Don't you?" She put one of them at my place. She's so nice. Her mama had us write everybody's name on a card so she could put them on the table where she wanted everyone to sit.

"Can't have everyone fussin' over what favor they want," she said. "This way we'll get everyone sat down prompt like when we're ready to cut the cake." That was a really good idea. I figured that'd be a good thing for me to do at my party come next year.

"I'm gonna do that at my party next year, Mz.Thompson," I said.

"Weren't you supposed to have one this year, honey? Seems like I remember that."

"Well, I was supposed to, but it didn't work out."

"I'm sorry, Lori Jean," she said.

"Oh, that's okay. If we get us any extra money, I get one next year for sure."

"That's nice," she said.

"So it's pretty for sure, I think. I mean, next year we ought to have ourselves some extra money. It's been a while. I reckon it's about time, don't you think?" I asked her.

"Don't see why not, Lori Jean. Mill's going strong right now."

"That's what I figure. Next year I'll have me a real nice party like this. And you can come and help me get the table ready, Carolee, okay?"

"I wouldn't miss it for nothin'," she said. I knew I could count on Carolee, her being my best friend.

"Yeah, next year I'm gonna have me a fine birthday party," I said.

We set up all the games. We played pin-the-tail-on-the-donkey. Carolee's mama had a prize for the winner who pinned it on closest to where a donkey's tail oughta be. It was a box of Cracker Jacks, which was a really good prize 'cause you never know, you might get the one has a ring in it. Never know. I tried real hard to win that prize, but once they spun me around I lost track of what direction that donkey even was and pinned his tail to the wall. When it come Darla Faye's turn, she peeked out under the blindfold. I seen her and she pinned that tail to Carolee's arm, only it didn't stay put, it just pricked her real good—drew blood even. Looked like to me it was on purpose, but I didn't tell Carolee. I didn't want to spoil her party none. She probably figured it out anyway 'cause she didn't cry or fuss. I think that's what Darla wanted 'cause she looked mighty disappointed when Carolee just giggled.

"That's my arm, Darla Faye. You lose!" Carolee told her and spun Clyde Farris around for his turn. He's real short and left-handed. He pinned the tail to the donkey's nose. It looked like a big drip of snot hanging down and everybody laughed. We was having ourselves a mighty fine time, we sure was.

Next, we played drop-the-clothespin-in-the-bottle. They play that game at every kid party I ever been to, so I should of won that one. I had me a bunch a practice, but Trudy Anne was invited and she always won it. If'n a body gonna have a party and play that game and Trudy Anne's invited, might as well not play it a'tall and just give her the prize 'cause she's gonna win. She's real good at it. Her ma lets her practice it whenever she wants, so she's like a champion player or something.

"Reckon we oughta play another game, Carolee?" I asked her before the party started. "'Cause Trudy Anne's gonna win this one for sure," I said. I was counting out all the clothespins.

"Well, Ma's got the prizes all wrapped and ready," Carolee said. "What else could we play?" I was thinking real hard about that when Carolee's mama told her to answer the door.

"Carolee, honey, April Dix is here. Take her present and put it on the table over there by the cake."

So we ended up playing the clothespin game. They give you five clothespins. Then they turn a regular kitchen chair around and put a milk jug on the floor below the seat. Then you kneel on the seat of the chair and hang your arm over the back of the chair. Then you aim each clothespin one at a time and try to get 'em to drop into that bottle. If it sounds easy, it ain't. You don't get to hang your arm over the chair very far; that'd be cheating. A body's lucky to get one in. Now Trudy Anne, I seen her plenty of times get all of them in, right through the neck of that milk jug. And it's a real skinny neck, too.

Sure enough, Trudy Anne, she won the prize. It was a shiny new red yo-yo. The string was all wrapped up in plastic still. I didn't feel so bad losing when I seen that. I don't got a yo-yo, but I tried Chester Britt's once and it weren't much fun. Mostly it laid on the ground and wouldn't come back up, even when I jerked on the string real hard. Except once, but then it come back up and smacked me in the head. Chester Britt, he can make it roll up and down that string like a window shade gone haywire. He's amazing!

"It's time for cake and ice cream!" Carolee's mama called out, and everybody run to the table lickety-split to find their name. Darla Faye climbed up on the chair at the head of the table with the princess hat.

"Darla Faye! Shame on you. You know that's the birthday girl's chair," Carolee's ma scolded her right away.

"You sit right here." Mrs. Thompson pointed to the chair next to Carolee and scooted her over. Darla took her place and stuck out her tongue at Carolee when Carolee put the princess party hat on. Darla's hat was the one that looked like the dunce's cap the teacher used at school. Carolee's ma had put a real nice circus hat out for Darla, one with bright blue polka dots on it. We switched it when her ma wasn't looking to the one me and Carolee thought was the ugliest.

"I hate you. You give me this dumb old hat!" Darla whispered to Carolee. I could hear her, though, 'cause I was sitting right next to Carolee on the other side. We put our hands over our mouths and tried not to laugh, but it come out funny through our throats. That made Darla so mad her face turned kind of purple. For once, we got *her* good.

Carolee's mama brought out the cake. It was Carolee's favorite. White cake inside with chocolate fudge frosting. Her mama lit the candles. We all sung that "Happy Birthday" song. Then her mama turned out the lights. It was so pretty. Carolee sucked in real hard and blew out all the candles. I didn't ask what she wished 'cause whatever it was, I wanted it to come true for her, for sure.

When her mama turned the lights back on, chocolate frosting was smeared all over Carolee's new party dress. A big gob of it covered up two of them pearl buttons.

"Carolee, honey. Look what you done to your new dress," her mama said.

Darla Faye looked at me and smiled like the devil hisself, if he'd been a girl. She was licking her fingers off, one by one, when no one was looking but me. I think I hated her more that day than when I wet my pants, but I couldn't be for sure.

Carolee started crying and run to her room in the back of the house. I run after her. Her mama did, too.

"I'll help her, Mz. Thompson," I said. "I reckon a best friend's real important right now, don't you think?" She just pressed her lips together and nodded and went back to the party.

Carolee had her dress off. She was rubbing at it with a wet washcloth. Made a terrible mess. That pretty dress weren't never gonna be the same. Carolee was crying the kind of tears where no noise comes out for a long time, but your chest moves up and down a lot. Then all of a sudden a big noise comes out. That kind a' crying. Which hurt my heart 'cause I loved Carolee as much as I loved Lexie Ann and Mama and MeeMaw all together. More even.

"Don't cry, Carolee," I said. "That's what she wants, don't ya' see?" I took my dress off and laid it next to her on the bed.

"You can wear mine, okay?" I said. Carolee looked up at me.

"It's not the same," she said.

"'Member all the times you admired it?"

"Uh-huh."

"Well now's your chance to wear it. And on a special day like today, it's perfect!" I said. "Let me wear your brown school dress. It don't matter none. I'm not the birthday girl." Carolee stopped crying then.

"Lori Jean, you're the most special girl in the whole world," she said. Fancy that! That's how I felt about her. We give each other a hug. Darla Faye wasn't gonna ruin the party, that's for sure. Carolee got her brown dress out of the closet. I put it on and she buttoned me up. Then I helped her into mine.

Carolee twirled round and round the room in my dress. It was even more beautiful on her. She was smiling and her eyes was sparkling like stars.

"I'm gonna love you for ever and ever," I said.

Her face lit up like one them angels I seen on a pretty store-bought Christmas card MeeMaw give me once.

"And I'm gonna love you back from heaven itself, Lori Jean, if'n I get there first," she said. "I promise."

chapter six

That fall MeeMaw caught the flu. Lots of folks got it, but MeeMaw was the only one in Roseflower Creek that died from it that year. She was near sixty-three years old, real wrinkly, but I wanted her to be with us no matter how old she got. Reverend Sims said she had a long, fruitful life and it was her time.

"Mz. Howard was a God-fearing woman. She was a fine Christian lady who helped anyone she could. She was a loyal friend. We'll all miss her," he said. He said some other words, too, but I can't remember them. They sounded right pretty, though.

I reckon MeeMaw would of liked it fine, but she'd of probably liked it a whole lot better if he'd skipped that part about her burning all the pancakes when they had the first hotcakes and pork sausage prayer meeting last year. That preacher repeated what Darla Faye's cousin Jimmy said when the blessing was being given. He'd started gobbling down his pancakes while Reverend Sims was still praying.

"Reverend Sims, you best pray o'er these *real* good," Jimmy yelled. "They's the worst cakes I ever tasted." When Reverend

Sims told that story while MeeMaw laid in her coffin bed, everyone laughed real loud, except for me. I knowed MeeMaw took her pancakes serious. If she was gonna laugh herself good, it weren't gonna be over her cooking, that's for sure.

Mama took it real bad when MeeMaw died. She let Ray move in right away that year and give him all the money in the jar MeeMaw'd saved up. They went out drinking and dancing, and they come back real late and made a whole lotta funny sounds in the night. Scared me to death. I told Carolee about the bed knocking into the wall and all that moaning and groaning.

"He's killing my mama, for sure, Carolee," I said. "He sure enough is."

"Oh, Lori Jean," she said. "You're so funny!" She scrunched her neck down and giggled real good. "My folks does that all the time! They's makin' whoopee."

"Whoopee?" I said.

"Uh-huh." And that's when she told me what Connie Dee told her about making babies and stuff.

"Grownups get all in a tizzy when they does it, Lori Jean. My cousin Millie Anne said it's like she went to the moon and back. She said she did a whole lotta screamin'. So don't be payin' your mama no mind. She might be yellin', but she probably likes it real fine."

"How can you be so sure about that, Carolee?"

"'Cause my mama's always got a smile on her face the next day."

"Well maybe she's smiling 'cause she done lived through it," I said. Carolee thought for a moment.

"No, it ain't your regular kind a' smile. It's a special smile. I think she likes it."

"Sure be nice to know for a matter of fact," I said.

"We'll just have to wait and see, Lori Jean," Carolee said.

"Millie Anne was fourteen when she found out. I reckon I'll jist wait 'til I'm fourteen and find out for myself," she said. "How about you, Lori Jean?"

"Ain't no sense in both a' us findin' out is there?"

"S'pose not," she said.

"That's what I figure," I said. "How about when you find out, I just take your word on it?"

* * *

That first winter after we buried MeeMaw, my ma got sick. Every morning she'd throwed up in the chamber pot she kept under her bed. After a while she got a bit better, but come one night Ray fetched a strange doctor to come around I ain't never seen before. Mama cried the whole day long 'fore he got there. Ray told me to wait in the bedroom and not to come out 'til he said to.

"Git yore butt in the bedroom and stay put, 'til I tell ya' different," he said. He come in not long after. We sat on the bed while my ma stayed in the kitchen with that doctor fella.

"How come you didn't fetch Doc Crawley?" I asked him.

"He don't do this kind a' doctorin'."

"What kind a' doctorin' is that?"

"Your ma's got a special problem. A lady problem. That's all you need to know." Ray got a real mean look in his eye.

"You don't mention this night, you hear? You didn't see nothin'. You didn't hear nothin'. You got that?" He grabbed my shoulder and dug his fingers in.

"Yes, sir," I said. But it was a lie. I seen that man. He didn't look like no doctor to me. And I heard Mama scream out in the kitchen, some plumb awful cries. I heard that man, too. He had a deep, gravelly voice.

"Don't move!" he said. "You move, it's gonna hurt all the more."

Ray kept staring at me. After a while Mama come back and laid down on the bed. Ray got a bottle of whiskey out and took a long swig. He offered the bottle to Mama, but she shook her head and rolled over onto her side and faced the wall. Then Ray left. I curled up next to Mama and fell asleep. When I woke up there was blood all over the bedclothes.

"Lori Jean, git up, honey. I gotta change these sheets 'fore Ray gets home," she said. I got up.

"Oh, Mama," I said, "we best fetch a regular doctor. That other one's done somethin' bad awful to you!"

"I'm gonna be fine. You go on back to bed now."

"But Mama . . ."

"Go on . . . it's nothing. Just a little blood is all. I'll be fine come morning," she said. Even so, I was mighty scared. I give her a hug. Her face was pasty white, and she was all clammy.

"Go on now. I'm fine. Just fine."

But she wasn't fine, not a'tall. I woke in the night to check on her. She was on the floor in a puddle of blood as big as me. Her nightie was all hiked up and all that blood was coming out of her private place. She didn't have her panties on, and I could see the fuzz down there she ain't never let me see before. Ray was asleep in the front room on MeeMaw's old sofa. I about woke up the moon I was so scared.

Ray stuffed some towels up against her bottom and fetched Doc Crawley. I know he come directly, but it felt like I waited three days' worth of revivals 'fore he got there. Doc took one look and said we needed an ambulance. We didn't have a phone. Time was a wasting, he said, so they did the next best thing. They wrapped her up tight in the bedsheet and put her in Doc's Buick.

"What in thunder went on here?" Doc Crawley asked Ray as they was tucking her into the back seat. I heard Ray tell him my ma took a coat hanger to herself.

"I begged her not to, Doc. Begged her. I went out for a piece and that's when she gone and done it. Found her like this when I got home," Ray said. Doc got in his car and tore down that dirt road that led back to town. I found out later he called for an ambulance there and it come and took her clear over to the hospital in Decatur. She near bled to death.

I don't know why Ray told Doc Crawley that lie about my mama and that coat hanger. That's plumb crazy talk. Why would she do something like that? I wanted to tell Doc when they was wrapping her up tight that if a coat hanger got took to her, it wasn't her that did it, more likely it was that stranger Ray'd paid money to, done it to her on the kitchen table. I wanted to, but Ray was staring me down good. His eyes was black as a hoot owl fixing to strike. I was sore afraid if I told, Ray'd call that man back once Doc Crawley left and pay him to hurt me next. I was a coward for sure, I was, but I forgived myself, 'cause a coat hanger poked in a potty spot sounded like a sorrowful way to die.

My mama made it. Doc Crawley said it was no small miracle, either. I listened through the walls the first night she got home. They's like paper. My mama was crying. It sounded like they was trying to talk soft, but it didn't do no good. I could hear every word.

"There won't be no more babies, Ray Pruitt. That's what this done to me."

"What's it matter?" Ray said.

"It's what you promised, Ray. Git married. Have us a baby. You'd settle down. You said, Ray. You said." I heard Mama cry harder.

"Shoot, Nadine, we can still get married. I kin settle down. I don't need me a baby to stop chasin' women."

"Is that so?" I heard my mama blow her nose. "What's it gonna take then? Huh?"

"Well to start with, it's gonna take us gettin' married."

"But we'll never have a young'un. Married folks s'posed to have a young'un between 'em. Brings 'em together." I could hear a sadness in my mama's voice I ain't heard before.

"More like brings 'em apart, as I see it," Ray said. It give me a fear in my chest when he said that. I remember thinking Ray might be right. My ma and pa had me between 'em and it sure didn't keep 'em together none. I musta pulled them apart.

My mama was still crying. I heard the bedsprings creak like they does when she rolls over towards the wall. Then I heard Ray's boots on the floor. The bed creaked a bit louder. He probably set down on the edge and pulled my mama back towards him to sweet-talk her.

"We're gonna get married like I said we was before any a' this happened. And I'm gonna be good to ya'. I am," Ray said. That sounded like one of his lies for sure.

"Ain't nobody else in this dad-blame town gonna take care a' ya', that's for sure." My mama didn't answer none that I could hear.

They told me the next day they was getting married when she got strong enough. Mama seemed happy about it. She was talking about getting a new dress even, and Ray said she could. Mama said it was a good idea; that it was time they settled down. Seemed like a dumb idea to me. Guess she figured Ray was gonna be a new man after the wedding. I couldn't rightly understand my mama's way a' thinking. Ray was a terrible boyfriend. How'd she figure he'd be any better a husband?

Even so, I wanted her to be happy. I was trying to figure out how it was I'd pulled my ma and pa apart so's I could keep from doing it to Ray and Mama. I thought real hard, but I couldn't think of what it was I done. Those years was mostly all a blur. I just remembered my pa's green truck. And I remembered the smoke coming out of the tailpipe all the while it roared down that dirt road getting away from us.

* * *

Bit by bit, Mama got stronger. All during that time, Ray never hurt her. Not once. I didn't hear no more sounds in the night, either. But then Ray, he stayed out most nights during that time. He'd come home some mornings reeking of perfume. At first I couldn't place where I'd smelled it before. Then I remembered. Connie Dee had some perfume like that. Connie Dee wasn't pretty like Carolee and she was fat, too. Took after their cousin Eugenia, Carolee said. After Connie Dee's boyfriend dumped her for Lou Anne Purdy, she took to wearing a lotta makeup when their pa wasn't around to see, trying to get some other fellas interested in her, I reckon. Mostly she got fatter and fatter. Then she started wearing a lot of that kind a' perfume I smelled on Ray. It come in a pretty dark blue bottle with a silver top. She called it Midnight in Paris.

"One whif a' this and a man will do 'bout anything," she said.

All that fat and makeup—she had that right. My mama never let on if she smelled that perfume on Ray. She was making plans for the wedding at the Rock of Calvary Church, up on the hill where we went every Sunday. It was all set for Easter time and the weather was near hot as summer. "A new beginning," Ray said. The year was going real slow. I was still eight, but seems like I shoulda been older.

I stood next to Mama that day while she and Ray stood

under the ivy trellis the church ladies strung up. He give her a gold band, put it on her finger and promised to love her and cherish her 'til he died. He was full of lies, that one. I think the preacher knew it, too. He stood back when the ceremony was over and kept shaking his head as everyone was wishing them well and congratulating Ray.

Even so, it was a fun day that day they got married. Everybody brought along a different covered dish. The church ladies set the food out on this long table the men carried out to the church lawn. They strung crepe-paper streamers from the trees, and they put these white puffy paper bells in the center of the table. It was a reception or something and the fanciest party I ever been to. Fancier than Carolee's even. Everybody from around Roseflower Creek come. Mz. Hawkins baked a two-layer wedding cake with blue flowers that matched my mama's dress. Mr. Hawkins took a picture of them he give 'em as a present. My mama's smiling real nice. Her eyes is kind of tearful, though. Happy tears probably, but could be sad, I guess, if in her mind she was looking down the road a piece. Still, it's a right nice picture. My favorite. When everything started going wrong for us, the sheriff took that picture and give it to the posse.

chapter seven

Come June, Lexie was almost ready to have her baby. I went with Melvin in his truck to get Lexie a present to cheer her up while she was waiting. What Melvin told me made it real hard to hate Ray like I wanted to. Melvin said their daddy was a real mean fella. Tried to work hisself out of being poor in Alabama and couldn't do it, so he drunk hisself to pieces trying to forget it. Didn't do a decent job of that, neither. He come home mostly and beat on their mama, and Ray, being the oldest, stood up for her real good and got knocked around hisself more than their mama ever did. Melvin said Ray was right handsome once, 'fore their daddy punched his face in plenty.

One night their daddy beat Ray so bad he couldn't make it out to the shed to pee and Ray, he messed hisself all night long. Melvin said their daddy whupped him bad in the morning for making a smelly mess for their mama to clean up.

"You know, Lori Jean," Melvin said, "Ray never let me take a beatin' when I was a boy."

"Not ever?" I said.

"Nope. Not ever. He always got in between my pa and me before it could happen."

That made Ray sorta like a hero, I guess. It made me feel a whole lot sorrowful for him, it did. 'Course that didn't excuse him from hurting my mama none, but I thought maybe it had something to do with why he kept doing it. Maybe my mama looked a bit like his daddy and Ray got confused when he drank all that liquor. I asked Melvin if'n she did. He said no.

"Baby girl, I never saw anyone looked like my daddy, praise God almighty."

So it was still a mystery why Ray kept hurting my ma and sometimes me. I reckoned I'd have to think on that a while longer 'fore I could figure that one out.

We went into town that day, Melvin and me, and bought Lexie some baby blankets and a package of little T-shirts that's for boy or girl babies. Lexie was feeling right pitiful, she was. It was so hot. We was having one of them summers where nothing grew big enough to brag about at the fair. Peach crop died. Corn didn't come in good and it cost a bunch along the roadside when we tried to buy it. Peanut farmers wasn't real happy that year, neither.

Lexie was having herself a terrible time. She grew herself a baby belly bigger than any I ever seen. She had a mighty hard time getting around much that last month and she wan't sleeping good a'tall. The heat got so bad I could hardly sleep myself, and I wan't sharing my body with no little baby kicking theirself around, trying to get out. I stayed with Lexie that night when we got back from Clarkston and put washcloths on her forehead. She said it felt so good. Kept me up most of the night, but I didn't have any school so it didn't matter none. I'da done it even if I did.

Melvin, he still had his job. He had to go to work in the

morning so he was fast asleep. He didn't drink hardly ever, just once ever' so often, so he didn't have no trouble keeping work like Ray did.

Early on the next morning, Melvin left for work about the time I was falling to sleep. I was just drifting off when Lexie Ann woke me up. She had a month left to wait 'fore she had the baby, but that didn't seem to matter much that morning.

"Lori Jean! Wake up!" Lexie said, and yanked the pillow out from under my head.

"Lori Jean, go on over to Mz. Hawkins! Tell her to call Doc Crawley and send somebody for me!" Lexie yelled.

I jumped out of that bed. Lexie had her hand under her belly and was holding it in place like that baby would plumb fall out if she let go. I was so scared it would, I felt the floor ready to leave me. My head told me to get moving, but mostly I just stood there staring.

"Lori Jean! Go! Go! Go!" Lexie yelled at me.

I run out to the kitchen. I still had my clothes on from yesterday, except for my shoes. I couldn't rightly 'member where they was. I was looking around for 'em when Lexie let out a holler like I never heard a'fore in my life. I looked up and she was laying herself down on the floor flat on her back, moaning something terrible. Water was running out of her bottom all over the kitchen linoleum.

"Lexie, I best not leave you!" I said. "I best not!"

"Lori Jean, if you don't go get help right now, I'm gonna kill you, right after I die havin' this baby, hear?" she said.

I run over to Mz. Hawkins in my bare feet, screaming bloody murder.

"Mz. Hawkins! Mz. Hawkins! Call Doctor Crawley!" I run right on into her house without knocking or waiting polite like for her to answer.

"Lexie's havin' her baby! She is! Right there on the kitchen floor!" I yelled. "Doc said it ain't time yet," I said, "but he musta forgot to tell that baby!"

"Settle down. Settle down," Mz. Hawkins said, and she grabbed her phone to ring up the doctor. Lexie and Melvin didn't have enough money for a phone yet.

Mz. Hawkins took care of everything. I don't know why Lexie didn't like her none. She run real fast for a fat woman and never even fell over—and her with those skinny little bird legs toting her whole body. She still had her nightdress on and her bosoms was heaving theirselves ever which way. I thought they was gonna knock her down for sure, but they didn't. She was already tending to Lexie when I caught up with her.

"Lori Jean, get some bedsheets off the bed and bring 'em here," Maybelle said. I done like she said and Maybelle scooted them under Lexie.

She had Lexie blowing air out of her mouth like she was blowin' up a balloon, or trying to. Mostly Lexie couldn't do it and was squawking real bad. Mz. Hawkins started yelling at her.

"Pant, Lexie! Pant!" she said. Then she changed her mind, I guess, 'cause she told her to do something else.

"Okay, push!" she said. "Push!" But Lexie just screamed.

"Aaaaaaahhhhhh! Aaaaaaaahhhhhhh!" But she must of pushed, too, cause Mz. Hawkins said, "That's it! That's it!" Then she said, "Stop! Don't push no more! Don't push!" It was mighty confusing, it was, but Lexie was just following along as best she could. She was back to blowing air out her mouth again. Maybelle looked up and saw me stuck to the floor like a stickpin.

"Lori Jean, go on now. Make yourself scarce. This here's woman's work," she said. She shooed me towards the bedroom.

"Go on," she said. "Go watch out the window for Doc

Crawley." Maybelle waved me off with the back of her hand. I stepped backwards towards the bedroom and inched my way to the doorway. When the frame smacked me in the back of the head I stopped and watched, even though she told me not to.

"Okay, Lexie," Maybelle said. "Now, push again. Hard! Again!" And Lexie did. She pushed so hard her face didn't look like hers no more.

"That's it! That's it!" Maybelle yelled.

Lexie looked like somebody just pulled her from the creek. Her hair was plastered flat down to her head. It was still red, but if'n you didn't know it, sure would of been hard to tell. It looked almost black and her face was so pale white she matched the chalk we cleaned off the board for Mz. Pence, if we was the lucky one got asked to.

Maybelle brushed her arm across her forehead. Her chest heaved in and out like she was the one doing the pushing.

"Look! Look here, Lexie!" she said. "You got a baby boy!"

I come full out of the bedroom doorway then and run over to Lexie. Maybelle had a baby by the feet. It was all blue. Sort of grayish black and blue, it was. It wan't moving or crying or nothing. Maybelle turned it over and rubbed its back real good, but that baby just stayed limp. I was getting real scared for it, I was.

Lexie wasn't doing too good, neither. She hadn't stop yelling. There was blood everywhere. That kitchen floor looked worse than the spot where MeeMaw used to chop up the chickens. Goodness gracious! All that blood from having one little old baby. That's when the floor disappeared right out from under me. And when that floor come back, it weren't a floor no more. It was a sofa. I was laid out with a sheet tucked all around me. Melvin was there.

"Baby girl, you had yourself quite a day," he said.

"Oh, Uncle Melvin," I said. "We had ourselves a baby and there was no one round to help us none."

"I know, sweet pea," he said. "You just rest now. Doc says you're gonna be just fine, goose egg and all."

"I wanta see the baby," I said.

"Well, you just rest for now, baby girl, okay?" Melvin said. That wan't hard since I hadn't slept none the night before. I was wanting to make sure that baby was okay, but a'fore I knew it, I was falling asleep.

"Is the baby okay, Uncle Melvin?" I whispered as I nodded off. "Is he?"

"Ssshhhhh," he said. "Go to sleep. Everything's gonna be okay."

My eyes were real heavy, but I remember thinking *the baby's not crying*. Matter of factly, the house was quiet as church.

chapter eight

I don't know for sure why Ray lost his job over there at the cotton mill. He coulda come in with liquor in him. Wouldn't be hard to smell it on his breath. Sometimes he drunk all night long.

Ray was a hard one to figure out. Sometimes he was so nice to my mama and me, it was like a new man moved into his body and just took over. Like that summer when Lexie was having her baby. She recovered fine from the birthing. And her and Melvin had themselves a set of them twins where you get two babies at once! They was almost identical, they was, 'cept one was a boy and the one that come out when the floor left my feet was a girl. Even so, I couldn't tell them apart, 'lessen their diapers was off. Lexie could.

Doc Crawley got both of them howling just fine when he got there and had my mama come over to help. Mama got Lexie to nurse them right off and they drifted on to sleep. Ray come, too. He was real jolly. Later when they woke up, he held those babies hisself.

"It's yore uncle Ray, little fella," he said to the one they named Irl. They named the little girl one Katherine Alice after

Lexie's mama. Irl wan't named after no one. Lexie just liked the name real good. Melvin didn't much mind what she called them. He said he liked the babies just fine and he trusted Lexie to give 'em a good name to take 'em through life. I think he was worried how they was gonna afford two of them at once. The mill was cutting back when no one figured on it, so Melvin was getting less hours every week.

Come Labor Day the mill had their regular year-end picnic for all the workers and their families. Noble Brewster, the boss man, said we could come since Ray worked most of that year 'fore they fired him. That was real nice of him, too, 'cause he didn't have to. They was having a dance for the big folks and everything. It was real special for sure.

They had lots of good food; watermelon for dessert, all you want even, and they had games and prizes for us kids. The gunnysack race that year was the one to win. They was giving away a new bicycle to whoever finished first. It was one of them two-legged races. You had to register who the contestant was and then your partner just helped you out. They didn't have to know who that was. Carolee and I was practicing a lot together. I didn't have me a bike, so I was the contestant. Carolee had herself a bike her daddy fixed up for her. She wanted me to win that bike so we could go riding all over together without me riding on the back of her bike like we always done. That was a real good idea, too, plus I wanted it bad. I never had me a bike before.

We practiced day after day, we did. With a gunnysack race, 'lessen you git good, mostly you just fall on your nose when you go fast. But we was getting better at it and the skin on our noses was healing up pretty good.

The day of the race we was surprised to see Darla Faye in line 'cause she had herself a fine bicycle already. But there she was, registered as a contestant and her cousin John Thomas was her partner.

We all lined up in a row. Darla Faye and John Thomas managed to settle themselves right next to me and Carolee. They was grinning ear to ear. Now me and Carolee, we was taking this race real serious like. We wasn't grinning at nobody, but we wasn't trying to be unfriendly or nothing. We was just concentrating real hard on winning 'cause a lot depended on it. We was real tired of riding double on Carolee's bike. We was sorely determined to get me one of my own, and this was about the only chance. Ray still hadn't found any regular work, just odd jobs and stuff.

The fella in charge of the race blew his whistle and we took off. Carolee and me darted away from that starting line so fast we was three feet ahead of everybody. We'd practiced for days on end pretending our ankles was locked together in the gunnysack. Both our legs was in and we just kept barreling ahead faster and faster. I sneaked a peek sideways and saw John Thomas and Darla Faye inching up next to us. They was almost neck to neck, so we plugged along faster. We was still a touch ahead of them and that's all it took to win. There was only a few feet left to go and we'd be at the finish line! I was so excited my heart was pounding out of my body and my spirits was floating somewhere up on a cloud. I was getting me that beautiful new bike! I knew it. I was inches away. Next thing you know, John Thomas took a flying leap trying to catch us and Darla Faye got plumb knocked off her feet in the process.

She went falling sideways right into our path. Carolee's leg stumbled over her in a heap and I come to a flying halt and landed next to her on my butt. Darla Faye jumped up and brushed herself off.

"Oh that's such a shame, Lori Jean," she said. "I think you

mighta won if John Thomas woulda watched where he was goin'."

My eyes was blurring over and I was real close to crying. It wasn't 'cause my butt was hurting, either, even though it was. It was for the hurt in my chest. Right then I thought of my mama. I'd done what she told me not to: counted on something 'fore its time.

"Lori Jean, honey," she said that morning, "don't go countin' on something 'til it's a fact. Okay?"

"Okay," I answered, but mostly it was just to be polite.

"I want you to win that race and get that bike more than I can tell you," Mama said, "but sometimes life is mighty cruel and won't give you what you want, even when you deserve it most." Yep, that's what she said that very morning. Now I remembered it good.

I looked up and saw Mama standing next to Ray. They waited for the man with the whistle to call out the winner. Then they motioned for me to come over to where they was. I got up and brushed myself off and hung my head down trying to hide my tears.

"I'm sorry, Lori Jean," Carolee called out. "It's all my fault," she said, and she started crying. Her tears got all mixed in with the sweat that done broke out on her face. I might not of noticed her tears so good at first, but they run smack into the dirt covering her face. We was both kinda grubby from running through the dust we kicked up.

"It's all my fault! It is! I shoulda known Darla Faye would try somethin' like that and stayed clear a' her," Carolee said. She was sobbing now. Like to broke my heart.

"She didn't want that bike, nohow. She just didn't want you to have it, is all," Carolee said. She didn't seem to care she was crying in front of everyone there.

"It ain't your fault, Carolee," I said. "Don't blame yourself none. How was we supposed to know?" Carolee was still on the ground. I sat right down next to her and put my arm around her.

"Besides, it might coulda been an accident," I said. "She might not of meant it none."

"She did!" Carolee said. "I know she did!"

"Well then, let's not let her see it bothers us none, okay?" I said. It was bad enough losing. I didn't want Darla Faye gloating over Carolee's tears. I helped her up, then rubbed at my knees. They was all skinned up. Carolee's was, too.

"Look! We got us some good battle scars 'least," I said.

"You gals sure enough do, now!" It was Ray. He and Mama was at my side. "We're right proud a' you both. Done real good, ya' did," he said. They hugged me tight. And Ray, he ruffled Carolee's hair. See what I mean 'bout him being so nice? Like a regular daddy.

"Shame you didn't win that bike, Lori Jean," he said, "but don't you worry none; we're gonna get you a bike, now, hear?" I wasn't real sure about that, but I nodded my head like I was.

"Shoot—you ain't never asked for nothin'," he said. "You deserved that bike and I'm gonna get you one! That's final."

It was like a new man moved in and took over for Ray. Ain't that something? He didn't drink no liquor or nothing when he was like that. He was going to these meetings where everyone said their name and how many days it was since their last drink. He was up to fifty-eight days. Me and Mama liked him real fine.

Mama and Ray danced and had themselves a good time at the picnic. Then we all rode home in the back of Melvin's truck, singing songs and being a family. There was stars out and a moon even.

"It's almost time for the harvest moon. It's almost full," Ray said.

"See, girls?" He pointed up at it.

"By the time that harvest moon shines down, I'm gonna have me a new job," he said.

"Then we gonna get you a bike, Lori Jean. And we gonna take your mama shoppin', too. Some new clothes, real pretty ones," he said. "Things is gonna be lookin' up for us 'fore long."

It was so peaceful looking up at them stars that night. I smiled my way to sleep. Ray must of carried me in the house when we got home 'cause that was the last thing I remember, Ray being so happy—full of plans—and that almost harvest moon just shining down on us. It didn't matter none that I didn't win that bike.

Finally we was gonna be a family. Have ourselves some happy times to look back on. Git ourselves one a' them futures—just like regular folks.

chapter nine

That year the town folks and some of the church folks, too, give Ray a bunch of odd jobs to do. Morgan Thompson, that's Carolee's daddy, give Ray fifty dollars to work on his tractor to get it in shape so he could get his field ready for spring planting. And he give him ten dollars extra to get new parts. Ray, he give that fifty dollars, all of it, to my mama! We had ourselves some fine groceries, we did. Bought us a ham roast and some bacon from old man Hawkins. Cost two dollars and fifty cents. Mr. Hawkins took thick slices of bacon, a nice pork shoulder roast and three pounds of pork chops right out of his smokehouse. It was all salted down good from when he butchered one a' his hogs that winter. Mr. Hawkins had a lot of big fat hogs to butcher and they growed fatter every year. Somes he sold and somes he kept. My favorite was Colonel Corn. He pushed all the others outa his way to get the corn. He was a real hog, that one. Right fine pig, he was. I liked him best ever since he won a prize at the fair the year before and Mr. Hawkins let me stand a'side him for the pictures.

We took them hog parts home. Come Sunday, Mama fixed us a fine dinner. We had black-eyed peas we left cooking in the pot whilst we went off to church. When we got back Mama made grits and ham hock gravy. We had biscuits and butter and some of MeeMaw's rhubarb jam we'd been saving from before she died. It was a mighty fine spread we had us that day. Lexie and Melvin come over with the babies. It was like a Thanksgiving and Christmas banquet and here it was just a regular Sunday after church when we sat down to eat it.

I sure enough enjoyed that good food. Mama roasted the ham with brown sugar and pecans on top like MeeMaw taught her to do. It was my favorite. I ate slice after slice of that pork roast; it about melted in my mouth. I ate 'til my belly nearly hurt something awful, which I hoped weren't a sin, but probably was.

I got to thinking how good pigs was to eat, which made me kinda sad 'cause they was so cute. That made me think about Colonel Corn, and I remembered the last time I seen him. It was right before Christmas when we got that cold spell that surprised us with snow. I never seen snow before. I never seen Colonel Corn again, neither. Mr. Hawkins butchered a hog that week it snowed. Good golly almighty! I knew right then we done ate Colonel Corn. I didn't sleep too good that night. I seen his snout a twitching and his pitiful eyes just a blinking at me. I tossed and turned in my bed. Finally 'bout dawn, I swore I'd never eat pork again if he'd just forgive me and let me git on with my life. I figured it was the least I could do, since I ate more of him than anyone else. In the morning 'fore school I told Mama about who we ate and how bad I felt.

"Oh, honey," she said, "he's in hog heaven by now, so don't you worry none about Colonel Corn."

I hoped she was right 'cause I sure needed my rest. The mark on the wall showed I'd growed another inch, and all that growing wears a body out for sure. After that I counted on that hog being happy wherever pig heaven was, and I figured if'n he wasn't, 'least he musta forgived me 'cause I didn't have no more trouble sleeping after that.

As a matter of fact, about that time it seemed like everything was going real fine. Ray was being so nice to us, my mama and me. I was getting real happy about having a stepdaddy like him.

It was spring the year I was almost nine. Carolee and me was helping her daddy with the plowing, following along one afternoon, picking up big branches a storm blowed down from the trees nearby.

"That's real fine work, girls," Mr. Thompson said. "Climb on up here. You can ride the rest a' the way." There was only a handful a' rows left to plow.

"I gotta get home, Mr. Thompson," I said. "Ray's takin' my mama and me to the picture show tonight." I was real excited. It was like a date. We was fixin' to get hamburgers and stuff 'fore it started. I stopped to see Lexie and the babies on the way home. That Little Irl was a handful. He was already climbing out of the crib and him not even a year old. Alice, that's what they called Katherine Alice, she couldn't climb good yet. She was a little bit younger than Irl, her being born last, so she wan't as good as him. He about showed her up in everything. But that little Alice, she just loved that Irl to pieces, I'm tellin' ya'. She followed him around everywhere, laughing and reaching out for him. Melvin and Lexie only had money for one crib, so the babies slept together, but I don't think they woulda slept apart, nohow. So being poor and only having that one crib suited them fine.

"Lori Jean, honey," Lexie said. "How'd you like to watch the babies for a while tonight? Melvin and me could get out for a spell."

"I'd like to, Lexie," I said, "but Ray's takin' Mama and me to the picture show."

"That's real nice. It's about time that man did right by you girls."

"Yes, ma'am. He's doin' real fine, he is," I said. "He's like a brand-new daddy. I think I could love 'im like a regular one even, 'fore too long."

"You gettin' enough to eat?" she asked. "I know he's not workin' regular."

"Well the church folks been helpin' with little jobs and stuff and the town folks, too. We gettin' by okay, 'til he finds somethin' regular," I said. "Mama's doin' laundry and cleanin' for Mz. Hawkins and I'm gonna help her this summer when school's out."

"Tell your mama, I'm gonna bring the babies by this weekend and visit a piece, hear?" she said.

But that weekend, nobody could come visit us 'cause we wasn't home. After I left Carolee with her daddy that afternoon, Mama and Ray and me got ready to go to the picture show. They was playing *Heaven Knows, Mr. Allison* with Robert Mitchum and Deborah Kerr. Robert Mitchum was my mama's favorite and Ray didn't mind her having a favorite movie fella none 'cause he said Deborah Kerr weren't hard to look at herself. We was fixin' to eat first.

When we got to the café, everyone was talking up a storm about a tractor accident. I was doing me some of that eavesdropping like MeeMaw always done. Seems a fella was plowing one his fields when the axle snapped off and threwed him clear to the ground. They took 'im all the way to Atlanta to the hospital there. They said he was gonna be all right. I was mighty relieved. Might could be somebody we knowed. Never know.

Dottie the waitress come over. She wan't really a waitress. She was the owner's wife, but she did the waitress work, took all the orders and stuff. I was fixin' to order me the Big Burger Plate. It cost ninety-five cents. It come with fries and coleslaw, but you gotta pay extra if you want a Coca-Cola.

"Go ahead, Lori Jean. Git yourself one them Co-Colas," Ray said. "Tonight we goin' first class all the way." He was in fine spirits, telling us jokes and stuff. He still weren't drinking no more and he was turning into a fine fella for sure. Mama and me was having a special time. We ordered our burger plates and Dottie brought our Coca-Colas while we waited on the food.

The menfolk in the booth by the corner was still talking 'bout that accident with the tractor that near killed some man.

"Reckon that might be someone we know, Mama?" I asked.

"Someone we know about what?" she said.

"That man them fellas is talkin' 'bout, got hisself near killed on a tractor. Reckon it's someone we know?"

"Lori Jean, stop listenin' on other folks. It's not polite," she said.

"Well I was just thinkin' maybe it could be someone we knowed and we should ask 'em who it was."

"We're out tryin' to have us a good time, Lori Jean," Ray said. "Let's just mind our own business."

"Well if it's someone we know then it sorta would be our business then, wouldn't it?"

"Quit, Lori Jean," Mama said and give me her evil eye. I guess she was worried I'd get Ray in a sour mood. I decided I best change the subject.

"What time's the movie start?" I asked.

"Oh, not for over an hour. We got plenty a' time," Mama said.

"Hhhhhmmm, Hhhhhhmmmm . . . ," Ray said. "Here

comes the chow." And there was Dottie with the biggest platters of food you ever seen. Burgers and French-fried potatoes was about my favorite eatin' foods in the whole world. Dottie put down catsup and salt and pepper.

"Anything else I kin get you, folks?" she said.

"That'll do us," Ray said.

We started eating and two more men come in and pulled up chairs around the back booth where them other fellas was. I recognized a couple of them but couldn't remember their names none. Burt Peters come out from the kitchen. He's Dottie's husband. He owns the place, and he does most the cooking 'cause he's real good at it. This big fella I never seen before was telling them mens that just come in about the tractor accident. Mr. Peters wiped his hands on his apron and sat down to join 'em.

I was thinking on whether it'd be okay to ask Ray if I could have me another Coca-Cola when I heard Mr. Peters say something that caught hold of my ear.

"They ain't told him yet 'bout Carolee," Burt Peters said. He was talking to the two that just come in. Now I 'membered their names, clear as church. It was Hoyt Anderson and Daryl Davis. They both owned farms up the road a piece.

"Doc thinks the shock would kill him for sure," Mr. Peters said.

I jumped up from the table we was at and run over and yanked on his sleeve. "What about Carolee?" I asked. Mr. Peters kept talking to them fellas.

"Mr. Peters, what about her?" I said. Mr. Peters turned around and looked me straight in the eye.

"What you need, Lori Jean?" he asked me.

"What about Carolee? Is she okay?"

"Why . . . she . . . she . . ." Mr. Peters was having trouble getting his words out. The men fellas all got real quiet and started looking round at one 'nother.

"Mr. Peters," I said. "Is Carolee okay? Is she?" I was getting a lump in my throat and a sick feeling in my tummy.

Mr. Peters turned his head to the side and spit tobacco juice into the can on the floor. That same floor was getting dizzy under my feet.

"She fell under the tractor, Lori Jean," he said.

"Oh no!" I said. "Well—did they fix her all up? Did they?"

"I'm sorry, Lori Jean," he said and shook his head from side to side. Now my tummy was really hurting. Carolee might be hurt real bad 'cause Mr. Peters had a powerful sad look in his eyes.

"They couldn't save her, honey," he said. "They tried real hard."

He reached out to grab hold of me, but he didn't move fast enough. The room spun me round and round like a toy top gone nuts. Then it turned itself plumb upside down. And if that weren't bad enough, the colors all about the room played tricks on my eyes. The yellow walls was blue. And the brown tables was red. Sparks flashed in front of my eyes like stars and the floor danced up and smacked me in the head. Voices screamed at me with lips stretched wide as a funhouse mirror. Words flew out of them voices; flung themselves towards my ears, stretched themselves like rubber bands strung out of a tunnel. They made their way into my ears, but they didn't make sense. First they whispered. Then they roared. First they was soft and then they turned mean. They screeched louder and louder. Still, they made no sense. Mean words, they was. They chased me. Slammed me down to the floor; sharp words, cut like razors into my chest. They dug out my heart. They squeezed out the blood, then printed their letters on top, right where it beat. They run all over the room, them words. They pushed in the walls and closed in the ceiling. They clawed and they poked. They spit and jabbed. They threw me into a cave; a black pit; a hole so tight I couldn't breathe. I heard them words. Bad words; crazy words; foaming-at-the-mouth words. They pushed their way into my head. Then I heard them good. I knowed what they said. I knowed what they meant.

"Carolee! Carolee!" I yelled back at them words. Too late. They pushed me deeper and deeper into the hole. The hole stunk like vomit and pee. I clawed to get out. Strong arms held me down. The room went all black and something in that blackness—something sharp and cold—took hold of my heart and cut a piece right out of the middle. I never got it back. Never. It was gone for good.

Just like Carolee, plumb gone forever.

chapter ten

They sent for Doc Crawley to come over to the café. Make sure I was all right. He give me a shot in the arm of something he had in his bag. Made me real tired and fixed my tongue so's it didn't talk good like it used to.

"Just take her home and put her to bed," he said. "She'll be fine."

But this time Doc Crawley was dead wrong 'cause I weren't never gonna be fine again. How's a body gonna lose their best friend in the whole world and figure on being just fine? Why, that's plumb crazy. Top of that, now I had me a tongue didn't work.

But Mama and Ray did what he said and took me home. They didn't get to see Robert Mitchum and Deborah Kerr on account of me and I felt bad about that, but what could I do? Could hardly sit and watch me *Heaven Knows, Mr. Allison* when Carolee was killed, my heart was broke in two, and my throat couldn't swallow 'cause a hard lump was stuck up in it. But that shot Doc Crawley give me sure helped. I knew Carolee was gone, but somehow I couldn't cry. I just laid in my bed all peaceful like, and strange as it was, I felt like everything was gonna be okay. Isn't that just the craziest thing? A shot that can do that to ya'—make ya' feel like the world's okay when it's flat-out ended. Goodness gracious, what'd they put in that shot anyway? I wanted to know 'cause I thought I'd probably need a whole lot more of it real soon. If it come in pills, I figured I could just take me one each day. Soon as my head wasn't so fuzzy, I planned on asking Doc Crawley about it. I did, too. I found out they got shots and pills and all kinds of stuff to make ya' feel like that, but he told me he couldn't let me have any more of it 'cause it was habit-forming.

"Well, if a body's gonna take it every day anyway, Doctor Crawley," I said, "what difference does that make?" He said people that takes it is drug addicts. Fancy that. They give me something to help me out when I learned about Carolee and they was fixing to make me a drug addict. It's a good thing I didn't take no more of that stuff 'cause I sure didn't wanna be no drug addict, even if life did hurt a bunch.

The day of the funeral I stood next to my mama to say goodbye to Carolee. They had her laid out in a wood box made up like a bed with her head resting on a white satin pillow. Her skin was a whole lot whiter than it was the last time I seen her. They had lipstick on her, too, and her ma never let her wear that stuff, so I figured she'd be pretty mad when she took a good look and seen what that undertaker fella did to her. Her hair looked real pretty, though. Wanda come and did it. She didn't want to, but Carolee's mama come to the shop and begged her when Lexie was gettin' a shampoo.

"Mrs. Thompson, honey," Wanda said, "I never worked on a person gone to the hereafter. You might should get someone with some experience, don't ya' think?" She looked up at Mz. Thompson whilst she was rinsing Lexie's hair and sprayed Lexie right in the face. Then she pushed a towel down on

Lexie's face to sop it up and poked her in the eye. Wanda sure was a bundle of nerves that day.

"I know you want that sweet little girl to look nice," she said, "and I jist don't know if I'd do a good job and all. . . ."

In truth, Lexie told me later, Wanda was scared to be in a room with a dead person. She only agreed to do it in the end 'cause Mz. Thompson didn't want no strangers touching Carolee that didn't have to and Wanda got a bigger heart than a scared heart and went on down to that funeral home and done it. Made Carolee look like an angel, she did. When we all showed up for the wake, Carolee's blonde hair was spread out all nice on that white satin pillow. Wanda put these cute little ringlets all around Carolee's face as a finishing touch. It looked real special, and I told Wanda so in front of everyone there. And I asked her to do mine like that in case I died 'fore her. She got mad and told me to hush up. Fancy that. Here I was giving her a compliment even. Mama grabbed my arm and had me sit down. Reverend Sims was in North Carolina visiting his sick mama, so this other preacher who wasn't a member of our church started the service with us singing "Shall We Gather at the River." Carolee didn't much like that song. I told that preacher before the service we should sing a marching song, but he wouldn't listen.

"'When Johnnie Comes Marchin' Home' is her favorite," I told him.

"Well," he said, "that's not even a church song."

"Well, it's a song," I said. "I reckon it'll be okay."

He ordered me to sit down pronto. Fancy that. It's her church. It's her favorite song and it's her funeral! Nasty old man.

* * *

We was gonna be nine years old that spring Carolee got killed. Me and her was just playing at the creek days before, throwing small branches from the chinaberry tree into the water, watching them float along, guessing whose would reach the bend in the stream first. We'd gathered up a passel of them fallen twigs, some as long as our arms. We stirred up a batch of mud cookies with one of them when we got tired of tossing 'em in the river.

We had ourselves a tea party on the grassy bank. Spread everything out nice like. Even invited John Benjamin. He was the only boy we let play with us 'cause he was real nice. Didn't tease us or pull our hair none. He was real polite and brought us flowers even. He was a whole lotta special things to us, he was. Only one thing wrong with John Benjamin. We made him up. But we pretended we hadn't whenever he was around. Treated him just like a regular person, hoping someday he might be. We told him how tall he'd grown and how handsome he was. That always made his cheeks red. I could see him there plain as pie, scraping the toe of his boot on the ground, his hands dug down in the pockets of his overhauls.

The day of the funeral we all went to the cemetery after the service. I stayed behind when everyone left. I told Mama I'd walk myself back home. She didn't mind none. She knew how sorrowful I was, Carolee being my best friend in the whole world and no one ever gonna be just like her ever again. I went off to find John Benjamin. It helped some being with him. Mostly the loneliness followed me around that summer. It was a root wrapped around my sadness, a stone that lay flat in my belly everywhere I went. It felt cold down there when I swallowed, even when I slurped down the chicken soup MeeMaw always said could warm the devil's innards.

When a memory of Carolee planted itself in my head, it cut

like a knife that slashed clear down to my chest. Nothing really helped it. Crying come easy, though. Seems tears was always spilling out of me like a water can sprung extra leaks.

"Carolee would be right sad to see you so sick at heart, Lori Jean," Mama said. "She'd want you to go on up to the cemetery and make peace with her, she would."

That's what I set out to do three long weeks after she left us. I picked a passel of wildflowers for her. I took 'em and scattered 'em all across her grave spot. Carolee loved wildflowers. I'd gone down to the creek earlier that morning and mixed up a batch of them mud cookies she loved so much, too. They was in my pocket. Some of them got broke apart on the way back to the cemetery, but I put 'em all out for her anyway, next to the flowers.

"Carolee, kin ya' hear me?" I asked. She didn't answer none.

"Kin ya'?" I kept talking to her, thinking she might still could.

"I know you're loving me back from heaven isself 'cause you said you would at your party that day. 'Member?" I laid out the mud cookies in a little circle for her. I put a daisy over the top of 'em. It looked right pretty. I hoped real hard she could see it.

"John Benjamin's here. See?" I held out his hand.

"My mama said you wouldn't want me to go around sad all the time. She said that'd make your heart cry. I figure she's probably right 'cause you was the kind of friend that always did nice things for me." I sat down next to her grave spot and settled in.

"I want you to know, Carolee, things won't never be the same now you're gone. But what I'm fixin' to do is not be too sad, okay? Just sorta sad. So when you see me smiling don't think I'm not missing you something awful 'cause I am. It's just I don't want your heart crying as bad as my heart's crying. Okay?" Me and John Benjamin got up to leave.

"And we're gonna bring you mud cakes and wildflowers every day, hear? 'Less it lightnings real bad, then we can't 'cause I best not chance getting 'lectrocuted." I patted the dirt spot where I figured her head was.

"Okay, then. We'll see you tomorrow."

I grabbed a few of them mud cookies. I decided to take them down to the creek in case she showed up like angels do. I knew she'd miss Roseflower Creek. It was our favorite spot. I wanted her folks to bury her there with Rose's flowers all around her, but they got some rule against it. Too bad, 'cause Carolee would of liked that much better. I knowed for a fact she'd of rather been over at the creek than up there in that old cemetery smack in the middle of them dead folks.

chapter eleven

On the last day of school we always got out early and the year Carolee wasn't with us no more wan't any different. I come down the road towards our porch and Carolee's daddy, Mr. Thompson, was pulling up in his truck ahead of me. He jumped down off the floorboard and propped hisself up on the one crutch he was still using for his bad leg got hurt in the accident and called out for Ray.

"Ray Pruitt!" he yelled. The curtains moved, but Ray didn't answer.

"You're in there!" Mr. Thompson thundered. "Don't be hidin' like no lily-livered woman."

"I'll fetch him for ya', Mr. Thompson," I said. I caught him unawares and he spun around.

"Lori Jean! You ought still be in school. This here's menfolk business."

"It's the last day, Mr. Thompson," I said. "We always get out early, 'member?"

"No—I—I don't rightly . . ."

Ray come out on the step.

"Wha's ya' want wi' me?"

He about fell off the porch. He reeked of liquor. He started back on that stuff the night of Carolee's funeral.

Mr. Thompson spat some words at Ray I couldn't quite make sense of. Then he grabbed a hold of the porch frame with one hand and swung his crutch wildly at Ray with the other. Ray didn't move fast enough and it caught him on the side of his head. Mr. Thompson was a really big man, bigger than Ray even. He had hisself fists the size of iron skillets. His muscles even bulged through his shirt all by themselves. The crutch knocked Ray to the ground. Blood was pouring out of his ear. Mr. Thompson stood over Ray.

"You killed my girl."

"Yer' crazy!" Ray shouted back. He scurried along the ground away from Mr. Thompson's boots. Mr. Thompson stuck his crutch under his arm and hobbled after him. Once he caught up to him he leaned down on his crutch and kicked Ray hard in the stomach with his good foot.

"Git up!" he said, but Ray curled into a ball like a possum. Mr. Thompson kicked him again. Ray moaned.

"Mr. Thompson! Mr. Thompson!" I called out. He looked up at me like he'd forgotten I was there.

"Ray's drunk, Mr. Thompson. It wouldn't be no fair fight now, would it?" Mr. Thompson's eyes was looking at me, but even so they was far away.

"Mr. Thompson?" I said. "Mr. Thompson?" He didn't answer me none. He just lumbered on back to his truck.

"He killed my girl. He killed my girl," he muttered. Then he climbed in that truck and drove away.

That's when I knew in my heart that what I didn't want to believe was possible probably was. Ray used my frame to get to his feet. He pulled on my arm, got up on one knee, placed a hand on my shoulder and pushed hisself upwards onto his feet. He staggered forward and lost his balance. He wobbled back and forth like a china plate spun on a stick. He toppled to the ground and pulled me with him.

I pretended to wipe the sweat from his face and he let me, but really I just smeared that blood comin' out of his ear all over him. I ground it in real good with the dirt and grime. It belonged on him. It sure did, so I squished that blood round some more on his face. It fit him, all right. You might not could see it, but blood was all over his hands, too. Carolee's blood.

"Thank ya', Lori Jean, honey," he blubbered. "Thank ya'." If he only knew, but he was too drunk to know anything.

But I knew. I knew Ray didn't fix that tractor right. And I knew Mr. Thompson was right. Ray killed Carolee. He may not of meant to, but he killed her just the same. When I looked over at Ray staggering to his feet, holding his belly, blubbering like a baby, my heart shoulda went out to him. But it didn't. There was no love left in it for him. There was just a deep sadness. Everything I wanted was gone. Everything. How could we ever be a family now?

chapter twelve

After that, Ray mostly did odd jobs and drank whiskey every night when he finished up. Mama kept on working for Mz. Hawkins and did laundry for some of the town folks. It kept us going. Ray managed to stay halfway sober for their wedding anniversary. They went to the May Day dance and he even brought my mama flowers when she was getting ready. She looked real pretty. Did her hair special and wore the ice blue dress she wore when the preacher married them in the church garden two years back. After the barn dance that night Mama went over to help Lexie with the kids. Irl, he was terrible sick and Lexie was a frettin'. Melvin come over to our place to set with Ray. Mama thought maybe that way he wouldn't get too drunk while she was gone. I went to bed, but had a hard time falling asleep. I was thinking back to how everything had changed on me the last two years. MeeMaw dead and gone to heaven. Ray moving in and marrying Mama. Carolee killed dead. I was beginning to feel a bit sorry for myself, I was. I heard Melvin and Ray talking through them paper walls.

"You made darn near ninety days, Ray. You coulda made it."

"Leave me be," Ray said. I heard the clinking of glass. He was pouring hisself another drink, most likely.

"It's a fact. You were doin' good!"

"Hhhmmmmm," Ray mumbled.

"Thompson's left the mill. Talk is he's takin' to drinkin' himself since the accident. I about got the fella took his place to give you a second chance, Ray."

"Fat chance a' that happenin'. The whole town's against me," Ray said.

"What's eating you? You full a' guilt? You got something to hide?" Sounded like Melvin was goading Ray good and that weren't like him.

"Who says I'm hidin'?" Ray said. "I'm drinkin'."

"What's got you drinkin' again? What'd you do, Ray?"

"Go on," Ray said. "Get on outa here."

"Talk is, you left parts on that tractor after Thompson give you money to buy new ones with," Melvin said. "That be a fact, now, Ray? Huh?" I didn't hear Ray answer.

"Talk is, you took that money, kept it for yourself, rigged that tractor. Killed that poor little girl . . ."

"God damn you, Melvin. Shut the fuck up!" Ray yelled. I heard a crash.

"Now, what you go and do that for, huh?" Melvin called out. "Now all your liquor's gone."

"You son of a bitch!" Ray yelled. I come flying out of the back room in time to see Ray take a full swing at Melvin. Melvin put up his arm and blocked it. He shoved Ray backwards. Ray tripped over his boots laid out on the floor and fell against the chair used to be my pa's and Ray'd claimed as his a long time back. There was a large splotch on the far wall where the liquor bottle had shattered. Pieces of glass was strewn all along the floor. The brown liquid left tracks on the cracked yellow walls where it made its way to the floor. Another mess for me and Mama to clean up, and no money for paint even.

Melvin hauled Ray up out of the chair by his shirt and held him tight. They was face-to-face now.

"If it's eating you alive, if that's what's got you drinkin' again, Ray, you best turn yourself in. Beg for mercy, boy, it's the only chance you got."

"You're crazy. I ain't done nothin'," Ray said.

"Oh, there's enough bad in you to a' done it, Ray. That I'm sure of," Melvin said. "Trouble is, there ain't enough bad in you to live with it!" He shoved Ray back down into the chair. That's when he seen me standing in the doorway.

"Git yer things, Lori Jean. Yer' comin' with me," Melvin said. "This one ain't fit to live with."

chapter thirteen

Mama and me'd been at Melvin and Lexie's place going on near two months. Katherine Alice and Irl were in the tub splashing up a storm. I was scrubbing them down real good. They'd been chasing the chickens after dinner, falling in the dirt mostly when they couldn't catch 'em. Had themselves a mighty fine time running after 'em, laughing all the way. Their birthday come while we was staying with them. Lexie had a real special party. Now they was two years old and here it were September already.

"Finish up, Lori Jean. You got school in the morning," Mama said and peeked her head around the corner.

"You best help me dry these little critters off, Mama," I said. "I no sooner get one dry, the other splashes 'im all wet again." There was puddles of water all over the linoleum. It was worn out in spots and most of the color was gone. What was left was gray. There was big cracks in it where the tub stood. The tub, it had these feet looked like lion paws. I liked to climb up in that tub myself. Hang my arms over the side and just wash my worries all away. Soak my troubles up good and let 'em run right down the drain when I was done.

Right then I was on my knees, hanging over the edge fixing to pull Alice out for the second time and I was about as wet as she was.

"Here, let me have Alice. You grab Irl," Mama said.

Alice smiled and rolled her face in the towel. I wrapped it round her and passed her off to Mama. She peeked out and giggled. Alice had the cutest dimples on her cheeks. Melvin was always saying he was gonna gobble them up. He'd make smacking sounds and go after her starting at her neck and she'd bury her face in his chest laughing so hard that it always started the rest of us laughing, too.

"Hhmmnm cook-eeeee, Nee Nee," Alice said.

"I promised her a cookie, Mama," I explained, "if she come outa the tub nice like."

"Cook-eeeee, Nee Nee, cook-eeeee."

"Let's get yer' nappie and yer' jammies on first." Mama patted her dry all over and headed for Lexie's bed to dress her.

"No, no, lay down, lay down, Alice." I heard Mama's soft voice coaxing Alice to be still and knew from the sounds of the springs squawking she was paying her no mind.

There was two things Alice liked to do better than chase the chickens. Run bare-buck naked through the house and jump on Lexie and Melvin's bed. I always laid her out on the small rug on Lexie's floor to dress her, else she never stopped jumping long enough for me to pin her didies on.

I patted Irl dry and laid him down on that rug now. He was getting tired and weren't no problem a'tall. He yawned and rubbed his eyes 'til they was little red half-moons.

"Cook-eeeee, Nee Nee." Alice had calmed down but hadn't forgotten her cookie. Mama's christened name was Nadine. But it come out Nee Nee when Alice said it. Pretty good for a baby.

I liked staying with them. We was kinda like a family. Ray hadn't come around once. It was real nice, even though there wasn't much room. I slept in a sleeping sack on the porch and Lexie made a bed up for Mama on the sofa they got at the secondhand store over in Decatur. It was dark green. The armrests was scratchy and all worn out and it had two cigarette burns on it, but other than that it was a real good one. Only cost ten dollars. With a sheet tucked around it, Mama said it was fine to sleep on. She would of said that though, even if it wasn't. Mama didn't like to be a bother.

"I think we ought to head on home, Melvin," she said that night after supper.

"Let him stew good and long, Nadine. Maybe he'll come to his senses."

"He may not have any left," she said. "The liquor mighta got it all."

"Give 'im time, Nadine. Let him realize what's important. He'll come around."

Lexie stared at Melvin and blinked. I don't think she believed it for a hot second. She looked around the small kitchen.

"It's just—well, we're in the way. . . ." Lexie cut her right off.

"Nadine, I don't rightly know what I'd do without Lori Jean helpin' out with the twins every day after school. She's a lifesaver, that girl."

"She could come help out, even if we moved home," Mama said. "She could come by after school."

"And don't forget the help she give me after supper. Why, it's like I been on vacation." Lexie patted her belly. Her and Melvin done made another baby.

Melvin was checking on getting them a trailer. They only had the one bedroom where they was and all four of them in it. It wouldn't do with a new baby coming. Now the trailer, it come with two bedrooms and a nice big living room. It even had its own furniture. Melvin was working a deal to help move and set them up after the owner sold them off his lot. They was all used ones, but real nice. I figured we should get us one and put it next to theirs. We'd be a real family, then. Ray could quit drinking and get hisself some work. We'd have the twins and a new baby next door. Yep, we'd be a whole family of relatives. We'd get together on Sundays after church, eat fried chicken and collard greens, buttermilk biscuits, and peach cobbler for dessert. I could see it and taste every bit of it. New baby and everything. Part of heaven right in Roseflower Creek. I might could have my own room even, if we got ourselves one a them two-bedroom kind. And those trailers all had a inside bathroom with a toilet. If only Ray could see what we could have. I might could forgive 'im for what he done to Carolee, seeing how he might not a meant to and all. Yes sirree, I prayed every week I could do that, forgive him. Every Sunday Mama and me headed off 'ta church, I said, "Lord, please help me forgive that no-good Ray, so's we can be a family." I prayed it on Wednesday night go ta' church meetings, too. And I asked the Lord to help Ray quit drinking. "And Lord," I said, "if'n you can't see fit to do that, could you just fix it so he throws that stuff up 'fore it goes down, instead a' after?"

He didn't answer me none, but I figured he was real busy and would get to me if he could. Melvin and Lexie was real busy about then, too.

Melvin, he was fixing to buy this 1947 Chevrolet automobile from a fella lived in Clarkston selling it to get hisself outa jail. He got hisself all drunk and smashed up the fenders when he run off the road and drove through old man Hawkins's chicken coop. Melvin got some replacement ones lined up and was gonna put them on hisself. The fenders, they was all different colors, but the car worked real good. Chevy engine. Melvin said Chevy engines was the best. If Ray straightened up, we could get us a Chevy automobile, too. I figured there was probably a fella drinking and banging his fenders at that very moment 'cause a whole lot of men folk drank too much. Sure thing, we could get us one of them Chevrolet automobiles, too. We could maybe see the USA, like Dinah Shore said to on the television. It was Mz. Hawkins's favorite show, next to *Ed Sullivan*. Sometimes she let me watch it with her. "See the USA in *your* Chevrolet." It was a regular family thing to do. If'n we had us a Chevy, we could be a regular family.

It didn't take long for Melvin to make them arrangements on that trailer. When Melvin said he was gonna do something, it was good as done. The day they moved in, me and Mama helped 'em. I lugged a box that was a bit bigger than me up the steps, then started down for another. 'Fore long I was mighty tired, but there was plenty left to do. Lexie couldn't help much. She was sick with that morning fever a lot of ladies get when they's growing a baby. Mostly Lexie nibbled soda crackers and threw up a lot. Then she drunk the ginger ale Melvin got for her down at Jonah's Crossing and throwed that up, too.

"Havin' babies is about as much trouble before they get here as after," Mama said.

I always thought Mama liked babies fine, but she said things that made it seem like she didn't when she was around ladies that was having 'em. Fancy that.

I about wore myself plumb out that day, hauling stuff up and down them trailer steps. I sat down on the last box I dragged in and watched Melvin wrestle the mattress up the steps all by hisself. Mama had the twins over at our place feeding them dinner, so I was supposed to do her part here 'til she got back. I needed to shake a leg, but my heart just wasn't in it. I kept thinking how nice it'd be if we was moving our stuff in and I was helping Ray and Mama get set up new like. I watched Melvin plunk the mattress down onto the box spring he'd hauled in earlier. They took up most of the space in the back bedroom. I pictured Mama and Ray scooting around each other in the morning, Ray putting on his work clothes, Mama pulling up the covers and patting the pillows into place. They was nice dreams, sure enough. I could see it all plain as pie. Still perched on that box I was resting on, I remembered what MeeMaw always told me.

"Lori Jean, you can't cross the creek by starin' at the water! Get a move on now."

That always got things rolling when we had work to do. I figured it might work for dreams, too. You just had to get 'em moving is all. After we carried the last of the boxes in, Mama come back with Alice and Irl. They was rubbing their eyes. It was time for their naps. Mama laid them down on the bare mattress and tucked a blanket around them. They curled up in little balls next to each other, butt to butt. They was so cute. Alice had her thumb in her mouth and the corner of the blanket looped around her fingers. She liked to rub the fabric back and forth against her cheek. Irl, he just liked to hug onto his teddy bear, which weren't really a bear, but a stuffed dog I made him that didn't turn out real good.

"Well, lookie here, Irl," Melvin said. "Lori Jean done made you a birthday bear." That's how it come to be a bear. 'Fore that it was a dog.

We tiptoed out of the room, Mama and me. I told her about my dreams.

"Mama," I said, "we gotta git ourselves a future. Git a nice place like this. And a Chevy car, too."

"You're dreamin', child," she said.

"Don't you got dreams, Mama?"

"I got dreams," she said. "They're old."

"Still, they're dreams," I said.

"Lori Jean, old dreams is like fire. Once the flame is out, there ain't much left but the memory."

"Oh, Mama," I said, "MeeMaw woulda never let that be so."

Mama was getting herself an ill temper and it come out in her voice.

"Well, MeeMaw ain't here no more now, is she?"

"Maybe so, but my dreams are. They're right here," I said and pointed to my heart. "And that's where they're stayin." I stuck my chin right up in the air so she could see I was sorely determined. That soft look come back in her eyes I seen now and then.

"Sure, honey," she said. "Sure." But it didn't seem like she believed it. I figured I'd have to make a believer out of her. I started working on a plan.

While Melvin and Lexie settled into the trailer, Mama and me stayed on at their old place. Rent was paid 'til the end of the month. Mama was hoping Ray would come round by then sober, with talk of a job. Truth be known, I was, too. It was the end of October. We only had us a few days left to go and we'd have to move back home for sure whether he was drinking or not. We'd run out of places to stay.

Melvin wanted Ray to come up in the world as much as I did. He kept getting on him about moving trailers for Mr. Jenkins. What a fine opportunity it was. A body could do real good getting started all over again. Peoples was buying them old trailers up like candy apples at a carnival. Mr. Jenkins had 'em painted all new like on the outside. Two men in white overhauls sprayed them with this hose that had silver paint come out the end. Lots of it sprayed right back on them and they was dotted with silver spots. Even their faces and their hair was spotted. Then Mz. Jenkins, she washed down the insides with suds and lye soap. They was pretty good inside then, pretty next to new.

I was real excited, but Mama didn't seem to be, or was hiding it good if she was.

"Oh, Mama," I said, "we're makin' our dreams."

She kept saying, "We'll see. We'll see."

"We gonna have us a new home in no time and then maybe that Chevy car and . . ."

"Don't go countin' chickens 'fore they're hatched, Lori Jean," she said. "The rooster ain't even near the hen house yet." Roosters, chickens, hen house. We was getting a trailer, what'd I care about a barnyard, nohow? Ray hadn't exactly said he was gonna work for Mr. Jenkins or nothing but Melvin said he wasn't giving up. I knew I could count on Uncle Melvin.

* * *

The circus come to town and he and Lexie told Mama they was taking me for a 'lated birthday present, since I didn't get me a party that year after all. I didn't much mind by then, since Carolee wasn't with me no more to help like we'd planned.

Barnum and Bailey joined up with Wringley Brothers or something and it was the greatest show ever on earth, they said. Imagine that! The greatest show ever on earth! I couldn't sleep for three nights straight 'fore we was fixing to go get our tickets. We had some other excitement that week, too. Melvin was still working days over in Decatur at the Scottsdale Mill, even though he worked for Mr. Jenkins when he got done there. The mill payroll got robbed sometime a'fore Friday morning when they was to give out the money to the workers. It was insured and stuff, so Melvin and the other workers got their money okay the next day.

Ray wasn't working there no more, so it didn't concern him none, but the whole town was pretty excited about the story in the Decatur paper. Melvin brought one and had me read it out loud. It was like a Bonnie and Clyde story for sure. Seems them robbers snuck in sometime during the night, fed the dogs raw meat and took the money from the safe. The paper said there wasn't any real sign the safe was even broken into. Seems the door was never locked to begin with. The paper said this Mr. John Allen Smithers who was in charge got hisself fired for not shutting it tight and locking it. And first they even thought he might of done it, but they decided not. The office lady said he had a habit of not locking up, on account it wasn't working real good. The combination or something stuck a lot, she said, and he couldn't get it open in the morning without cursing. They never been robbed a'fore, Mr. Smithers said, so he just kept leaving it not quite shut.

It was a real fine story. The lawman investigating it said there was over ten thousand dollars took and a reward would be posted of five hundred dollars for getting it back. Lots of folks was hoping to find a way to help the law out and collect that reward, but one of them lawmen fellas said the culprit was probably clear to Alabama by now and not to count on it. That got the sheriff mad. He said they didn't know the likes of his county and he'd catch 'em sure as church.

chapter fourteen

"Mz. Hawkins," I said, "they got a five-hundred-dollar reward for catchin' them robbers. Fancy that." It was Saturday. I was helping her fold the laundry. She give me ten cents an hour and I had me thirty cents due already and it wan't even twelve o'clock noon. Mz. Hawkins always paid Mama more. She was supposed to help that morning. We sure needed the money, but she went with Lexie Ann. They took Little Irl to the doctor in Decatur since he wan't no better. He had us all a bit worried, but Melvin said not to fret none.

"Young'uns is always gettin' sick," he said. So I stopped fretting 'cause he knew just about everything, Uncle Melvin did. But Mama and Lexie Ann was still worried and had creases in their foreheads when they leaned over him to check his temperature.

"That's a right nice amount, Lori Jean," Mz. Hawkins said.

"Ma'am?" I said, thinking she meant the money she was paying me for helping, which I was sorely grateful for, but even so, it didn't seem like much a'tall.

"That reward money, a right nice amount."

"That it is," I said. "Somebody was to get that, they'd be rich for sure."

"Right nice sum," she said.

"I'd sure like ta' git that reward money and give it to my mama," I said. "Git us a really big trailer and everything. That's what I wish."

"If wishes were horses, Lori Jean, beggars would ride," she said real sassy like.

"I reckon," I said, trying to be respectful like MeeMaw taught me, but I stuck my tongue out when she turned away, not being able to help myself none. I folded up a pair of her undies and put 'em on top of the laundry basket, then started on another pair. Them bloomers of hers was big as a cow's butt. I hoped God would forgive me for noticing.

She give me lunch, fifty cents and an extra dime I didn't do no work for, before I left, so she weren't all bad. Matter of factly, Mz. Hawkins could be right nice when she had a mind to be.

Seeing as our place wasn't too far off, I decided to go and see what Ray was up to. But first I wanted to sit with Carolee at her grave spot. I stopped at the creek, took my shoes and socks off and mixed up a batch of mud cakes. I loved how that clay squished between my fingers all gooey like. I stuck my toes in the muck, too. Then I made up a nice stack of them dirt cookies for Carolee and carried them on up to the cemetery. By the time I got done visiting it was getting late and the sun was setting fast. I went back down to the creek to wash up and get my shoes. One of them was there on the bank of the creek stuck in the dirt where I left it. The other one was nowhere in sight. I looked everywhere. Did a coon carry it off? Did it slide down into the river? It didn't much matter. Either way I was in bad trouble. They was the only ones I had. That's mostly why I took 'em off in the first place, so's they wouldn't get so muddy. I looked and looked. My stomach tied itself all up in knots tighter than one a' them mummies Mz. Pence showed us in a 'cyclopedia book.

I run all over that creek bank searching for that shoe. By then it was near dinnertime for sure. My stomach started growling and my eyes started watering. I was ready to plumb give up. I really didn't want to leave without my shoe, but it was getting dark, and the hoot owls was making noises in the trees. Then I heard some rustling in the tall grasses. The creek was moving a bit swifter over the rocks now that evening was closing in, making its own scary noises.

I went to the edge of the water for one last look, praying my shoe would appear. It didn't, but something else did, right out of nowhere. One of them snakes! Looked to be a black racer. Them kind ain't poisonous, I knew that much, but I don't like snakes. It slithered past my bare feet and slipped into the dark water. I took off running, but I didn't make it too far before I took a tumble. The mud patches I'd made earlier baking them dirt cookies tripped me up. Now my clothes was a sorrowful sight. I got back on my feet and headed to our house. Maybe Ray was out drinking and I could clean up there 'fore Mama saw what shape I was in. I hung on to the one shoe I had left, not knowing how it'd be any good to me now, but wanting to have something to show for my efforts.

A cold spell had settled in that last week of October. Set a record for Georgia, they said. At school Amos Moses Johnson even fired up the coal furnace to take the chill off when the principal told him to.

It was getting darker. The sun had sneaked off and the wind picked up speed. It blew faster than I ran. It zoomed ahead of me and smacked me in the face. I made my way out of the woods and onto the dirt road that led to our front porch.

I hoped the house would be dark, that Ray would be gone

and I could rest and clean myself up before I went back to Lexie and Melvin's old place, where Mama was waiting on me. Seeing the lights pouring out from the windows, I knew Ray was there and hoped even harder he'd be sober and in one of his nice moods, that he'd help me, maybe come with me to tell Mama, to say it didn't matter none about one old dumb shoe, that he had hisself a new job, paid good money, and we could get all the shoes we wanted. I prayed that real hard.

The closer I got, the brighter the lights got. I'd never seen our house so bright. Like Christmas, only brighter. I didn't even know we had enough lights to make it that bright. That's when I seen it wasn't lights a'tall. It was fire! Flames whipped out from the windows and poured from the front door.

"Ray!" I yelled. "Ray?" He didn't answer. I stepped onto the porch. The boards burned my bare feet and hot ash from the flames scorched the front of my hair. I knew I'd be in all kinds of trouble if I went in there, so I ran around to the back. The door was open and that's where I found Ray, sprawled on his stomach, his head twisted to one side. His fingers was wrapped around an old flour sack, black with soot, the edges burned and ragged. Ray's face was burnt bad, but his hands was worse. I heared him breathing, but not the way he breathed the last time I seen him. He breathed like a paper sack with holes in it, whistling and rattling.

"Ray, get up! Get up!" I leaned down and yelled in his ear. He wouldn't answer. I drug his arms over his head and pulled him hard as I could. He didn't budge. Splinters of wood tore into my toes. I yanked at him harder. He moaned real good.

"Ya' gotta help me, Ray! The fire's fixin' to git us both," I said. Which weren't no lie, neither. The flames was moving into the kitchen from the front room. They'd already burned out a corner of the ceiling. It come crashing down with a *whoooooosh*. Nearly scared me dead.

"Come on, Ray! Come on!" I screamed at him, but I couldn't get him to help me none. I went around to his backside to try and twist him about by his feet. The fire'd moved into the kitchen and it weren't long before the flames got hold of the back of my shirt. I felt hot fingers bite into my skin and grab hold of my hair. I wanted to run from that house as far and as fast as I could, to run and never look back. Something inside me said if I run, I'd die for sure. I laid on the floor next to Ray and rolled to the door. Over and over I rolled back and forth between him and the door. Smoke poured from my shirt and my hair. This bad stink come pouring from my head. I reached up and found the fire had give me a haircut. But I had no time to worry about that. Now the fire was done with my hair it was coming for the rest of me. My hands was growing these blisters, hurt something awful. Somehow I got on my knees and pushed myself back onto my feet. Bits of skin was peeling off my face, my clothes was half burned up, and my arms was near black. I screamed for someone to come help us.

"Somebody!" I yelled. "Heeelllp! We needs help!" No one answered. No one a'tall. It was up to me, and that was a real sorry fact 'cause I wan't doing a real good job of helping us none. Then I remembered God might could help us if'n he had it in mind to.

"You gotta help me git Ray outa here, God, or he's gonna die," I said. I jerked Ray's legs around to the door and tried to drag him down the back steps, but he was just too heavy. The fire was licking at my bare feet, turning my toenails black. "Is that what you want?" I asked. "Do you want him to die?" He must not of wanted him to 'cause the next thing I knew I done drug Ray right out of that kitchen doorway lickety-split. I had strength in my arms come from Samson or somebody kin to him for sure. I was David and the fire was Goliath. I was David and I won. I got Ray out onto the stoop and pushed him a good one right over the edge of the steps and down onto the ground. I drug him clear away from the house. The flames shot out of the windows and swallowed up the rest of the porch. What was left of the house weren't a house no more. It was a stick thing with no walls. The edges was all that was left and the fire was eating those parts up fast. Heat come at us as the flames got madder. I drug Ray farther and farther from what was left of our house. I drug him 'til I couldn't walk no more and fell down next to him in the dirt. The cool air stung the burned skin on my back. My eyes burned all blurry. My nose choked trying to get air, and I was coughing and gagging somethin' awful. Ray wasn't moving none, but air still rattled out of him. His fingers still clutched the flour sack. Bits a' burnt green paper was coming out of the top. I pulled it loose from his hand, and I shouldn't a' done that 'cause his fingers was black and clear melted into the folds. When I yanked that flour sack loose, some of the skin on his fingers pulled clean off with it.

"I'm sorry, Ray! I'm sorry!" I said, but he just laid there. More green bits flew out from the top of the sack. Some of it wasn't burnt at all. Money. It was money! More money than I ever seen in my life.

"Where'd Ray get all this money?" I said right out loud. But I knew. Only one place he could git hisself money like that.

"Good Lord," I said, "don't let me be right where he got all this money." But I knowed. I knowed for sure. I leaned over and threw up some yellow stuff. I didn't know if it was the smoke making me sick or the truth, but I puked 'til nothing more come up.

I checked myself over to see if I made it. My toes was crusty as old bread, my arms black as burnt toast, my hands was all puffed up and blistered, but 'least I was alive. Ray lay at my feet not looking like he was. I could still hear that funny breathing sound coming from his chest, though, so I knowed he was for the time being. I had to run quick and get some help, but first I had to hide the money. No telling why he took it. Most likely he was crazy out of his head with worry and drink, what with Mama leaving him and all. He didn't even know how to cook. Probably went nuts. I was sure when he come to his senses he'd want ta' give it back, make it right, git that job with Mr. Jenkins, make us a regular family. I was sure he would, if he lived. I hid that money in case he did. I figured I'd find a way to git it back later. I had to.

Ray done stole the payroll. He was goin' to hell and the chain gang for sure, Mama and me along with him if I didn't get that money back to the mill.

chapter fifteen

Come winter we had our share of problems and a right bit of somebody else's, too. That day our house burned down, Mama and Lexie was over at Decatur Hospital seeing about Little Irl when the ambulance come took Ray over to Grady.

"That's the best hospital for burns, Lori Jean," Mz. Hawkins said. "Couldn't do no better in Georgia."

Which were a good thing 'cause Ray near died and wasn't out of the woods yet. His face was burnt real bad; his hands, too. But his lungs was burnt the worst. They had him in a 'tensive care place. Mama could sit with him, but she had to put special hospital clothes on and paper shoes and a paper cap over her hair even, on account of Ray couldn't be round no germs a'tall. Mama said he was in terrible pain and they give him these shots to help some when it got at its worst.

"Why's it hurt so much, Mama? You'd think the pain would get better by now."

"They gotta peel the dead skin right off a' him, Lori Jean, so they can graft new skin on, honey." Later I heard Mama and Uncle Melvin talking.

"He don't remember the fire, Melvin. How it got started or nothin'. I think he's lost his mind."

"Shoot, Nadine. He's out of his head with the pain is all. Once they git them skin grafts all finished, he'll be a new man."

"I don't know . . ."

"He might end up a sober one before it's all over," Melvin said. "There's no liquor in him now."

"Maybe so, but they got him plumb shot full a' painkillers. I read me somewhere that kin be just as bad."

"You worry too much, Nadine. You gotta look on the bright side."

"I guess."

"I got Jenkins talked into givin' Ray full-time work soon as he's ready."

"His hands is all burned, Melvin. How's he gonna move them trailers?"

"They'll heal."

"Hope you're right. We gotta get our own place, Melvin," Mama said. "With the baby almost here, there's no room for Lori Jean and me. It ain't right, our being in your way."

"I'm working on that. Jenkins got an old trailer needs work. It'd be right perfect for starters. Set it up right here next to ours," Melvin said. I heared him with my own ears, I did! We was getting us a trailer. Probably nothing fancy like Melvin and Lexie's, but still it'd be ours. I sure hoped Ray'd heal up good, get to work, and show Mr. Jenkins he could pay on that trailer right regular.

Mama said Ray didn't remember about the fire. I wondered if he remembered about the money. I hoped not. I dragged that sack behind the outhouse before the ambulance come that day. It was still there, buried under as much dirt and scrub brush as I could muster to cover it with, being my hands was all tore up and bleeding from the fire. I was gonna move it to a good hiding spot, soon as I thunk up one. Then I was gonna find a way to get it back to the Scottsdale Cotton Mill clear on over in Decatur. I even had a note all writ up telling them the person who took it near died from pain in a fire and was plumb full of sorrow probably, too, if'n they could only remember and realize what they done when they was drinking too much whiskey. I asked 'em to forgive him like the Bible says to 'cause he weren't really a crook; he just didn't have no money, so's he took theirs in a weak moment. I told 'em how me and my ma's whole rest of our life depended on it, and we hadn't done nothing so's we'd appreciate it real kindly if they'd forgive the one done it. I didn't sign my name, though. I was a coward for sure. But I reckoned they'd be so glad to have their money back maybe they wouldn't notice or care none.

I planned to put that note in the money sack and set it outside the back door at night when no one would see me. Trouble is, it was 'least ten miles over and ten miles back, so I had to work me a plan. All during the time my back and hands was healing up I worked on thinking me up a plan, but my brain couldn't think one up. I talked to Carolee at her grave spot even, hoping that would help me, but it didn't.

I healed up pretty fast. Turned out I weren't hurt real bad from the fire, even though it looked like I was. My hair got burned good and Wanda cut it off 'cause she said I looked like Orphan Annie. I didn't know that girl none, but I felt right sorrowful for her on account of her hair being burnt up like mine and her being a orphan to boot. Now I had me a bowl cut; looked like one a' them boys. If that little orphan girl looked like me, she was one pitiful sight 'cause I looked like the dickens, I'm tellin' 'ya.

The part hurt the worst was my fingers. They was blistered bad, but the nurses fixed them up at the hospital and the doctor bossing them around sent me home that same day. My back got burned some, but that same doctor told me I'd probably not have any scars from it. Fancy that.

All during that time Mama was plumb wore out worrying about Ray healing up. She was fussing on Lexie and Irl, too. Lexie wan't supposed to be having a hissy fit about anything, her growing the new baby and all, but Irl's fever, it got real bad so they took him on back to the hospital. He just got worse 'stead of better. He couldn't breathe even. They took him over to Grady Hospital in Atlanta where this special doctor who only takes care of kids, and he told Lexie and Melvin that Irl got the terrible virus kids was getting all over the land and his lungs was paralyzed. Polio! That was the scariest word in the whole world for folks with little childrens. Doctors was going plumb crazy trying to find a vaccine or something and one of them, he said he found one. Whatever it was he found, he put it in these tiny little bottles and they started shipping that stuff all over the place. Mz. Pence said we was all gonna get vaccinated for it at school as soon as more of that stuff made it to Georgia. They run out. A really good doctor named Jonas Salk is the one found it and he got a prize for it and everything. I think them doctors had theirselves a contest over who could find a vaccine first. All of them wanted to be the one to win the prize. Then they'd get famous, too, 'cause that Jonas Salk doctor, he got hisself famous for sure. He was in the paper all the time.

What he done was take some of that virus he found and give it to these monkeys and growed it in their bodies. Then he got that virus out of them monkeys somehow. Guess he made 'em throw it up or something and then he cooked the virus up while it was alive, I think, and then he put it in these little bottles and some nurses stuck a needle in the end of them bottles and got the medicine out so they could stick us good in the arm. I read all about it myself in the paper, but most of it was pretty confusing, so don't hold me to none of the facts.

Cooking up that virus and putting it in a needle to shoot into my arm scared me worse than just taking my chances.

"I ain't gonna git me one a' them shots, Mama," I said. "They done took that polio they give them monkeys and cooked it down 'til it fits on needles. Now they wanna stick them same needles got that polio on it, right in ta' our arms."

"Oh hush, Lori Jean," Mama said. "Them doctors know what they're doin'."

"I don't know," I said. "Sounds right stupid to me. MeeMaw said somethin' don't make sense, be careful, it's probably a duck."

"Lori Jean! What in the world are you talkin' about?" Mama said.

"I'm talkin' 'bout that polio medicine they cooked up and what MeeMaw said about them ducks."

"What in thunder?"

"Don't you 'member, Mama? MeeMaw said if it looks like a duck, talks like a duck, must be a duck."

"Well, she weren't referrin' to no polio vaccine."

"Well, she was talkin' 'bout usin' common sense to tell what was what, that's for sure," I said. "And I don't rightly know if them doctors know what they's doin'. So alls I'm sayin' is, I'm not havin' me one a' them shots, 'til they do."

"You're takin' that shot, Lori Jean, and I don't want ta' hear no more nonsense, ya' hear?" Mama said. "You want to end up in one of them iron lungs? Stuck in a long metal tube with jist your head stickin' out? Is that how you want to spend the rest a' your days? Huh?" she said.

Since she put it that way, I reckoned I best git me one of them shots. That doctor fella, Jonas Salk, he might could know what he was doing. He got hisself a prize and everything. Maybe if they woulda had some of that medicine ready for Little Irl he wouldn't of got so sick. Later that week they put him in that iron lung. Lexie got so hysterical the doctor give her a shot so's she wouldn't go having the baby right then and there.

That night I seen a picture of one a' them contraptions in the *Decatur Daily Press* Melvin brought home. It was terrible. The picture was kinda fuzzy, but I could still see it pretty good. It showed a little boy no older than Irl stuck in a long silver thing, looked like a bullet. His little head poked out one end. He had light curly hair and nice pudgy cheeks, but the saddest eyes I ever seen. The headline said MARCH OF DIMES TO AID VICTIMS. The article said to give everything you could when the volunteers come to the door. I only had me seven dimes from helping Maybelle, but I put 'em in a jar by the front door, so's I'd be ready when they come. I wanted to call the paper and tell them to please send the March of Pennies people, too, 'cause I had me a whole fistful of pennies. I wanted to let them know lots of folks round here don't have theirselves many dimes left once they buy groceries, but most got plenty pennies they might could give. I set out for Mz. Hawkins's place so's I could use her phone to call 'em, but it wasn't working, so I couldn't. Somebody pulled the phone line off her house and it weren't fixed yet. She showed me where it connected right up near the porch and where somebody pulled it out. She was real mad about it.

"When I get my hands on who done it, Lori Jean, I'm callin' the authorities, I am!" she said. I knew she would, too. She called the law Halloween when Stubby Painter and

Clarence Jackson egged her windows after she wouldn't give 'em any candy. She told 'em to go back to their own kind for candy and stay away from white folks' houses. The law come to get 'em, but Mz. Jackson, Clarence's ma, she talked the sheriff out of taking them in when she promised to wash Mz. Hawkins's windows for free. She did the inside, but Odell Jackson, her husband, had to do the outside and he weren't none to happy 'bout it. I think he would of rather they hauled Clarence on off to jail. He didn't like Clarence much. Odell and Miss Pearlie had themselves about twelve kids. Every time I seen Miss Pearlie she was having herself another baby. I figured she must really like kids or something, but Mr. Jackson he sure didn't like Clarence none. He whipped him bad all the time, he did. He whipped him with a cat-o'-nine-tails for throwing them good eating eggs at Mz. Hawkins's house, which weren't no surprise. Sometimes Mr. Jackson whipped Clarence for no reason a'tall. Sometimes just 'cause he didn't like the grin on his face, Clarence said. Clarence had these scars all over his back on account of those whippings.

"Mz. Hawkins," I said. "I sure hope it weren't Clarence Jackson done it. He been whipped so bad by his daddy, he got scars all over his back."

"If that boy's got scars, he must have earned them," she said.

"I don't think so. Clarence said sometimes his daddy whips him jist 'cause he don't like the grin on his face," I said.

"Well, there you go, Lori Jean. That boy give his daddy some smart-mouth grin, he ought to be whipped. Teach him a thing or two."

"No ma'am," I said. "He weren't bein' smart. He was jist bein' happy."

"Is that so? Is that what he told you?"

"Yes, ma'am."

"And you believed him?"

"Yes, ma'am."

"Lori Jean, don't believe the half a' what you hear from them kind a' folks."

"But Mz. Hawkins," I said. "Them's right nice Christian folks. Go to church and everything. They's jist black, is all."

"Church indeed! You call that clapboard shack they do their jive jumpin' in a church?" I didn't answer. I didn't mean to get Mz. Hawkins all in a tizzy over white folks and colored folks. Seems people in Georgia was always having themselves a hissy fit over what color a body's skin was. I only come by to use the phone to call the paper on account of the pennies I collected. I reckoned people collecting money didn't much care what color a body's hand was that passed it to them. So why in thunder did it matter so much the rest of the time?

I decided the thing to do was put them pennies in a separate jar and keep 'em next to the dimes, case them March of Dimers would take those pennies and pass 'em on. So that's what I did. I put them in a jar of their own and left 'em by the door.

Weeks went by and Irl never got better. We finally got some of that polio vaccine at our school. They lined us up in a row to get our shot. Some of the kids cried and carried on when they stuck the needle in their arm. Made me lightheaded when my turn come. I gritted my teeth and shut my eyes so tight, I seen them star things like when ya' bump yer' head. It was over 'fore I knew it. Shucks, it weren't near as bad as the bee sting I got down at the creek last summer. Even so, I was glad it was over. The next day I felt a bit feverish and Mama kept me home from school. The nurse who give the shot said some of us might feel a bit poorly and she was right. I didn't even want to eat anything the next day, and here Mama made biscuits dripping in honey. She weren't too worried about it, 'til Melvin come home from Mr. Jenkins's with the evening paper. Then she got near hysterical.

One a' them batches of polio medicine they mixed on up was a bad one, and that one give two hundred fifty little children polio when it was supposed to protect 'em from it. And it killed eleven of them dead already! Fancy that. Here it was supposed to help 'em not get it and it give 'em the polio for sure. It was terrible; in all the papers day after day. Made me plumb afraid Georgia got a bad batch, too, and I was probably getting that polio any day. I went to school and pretended I was fine so's not to scare Mama, but I knew my days was numbered for sure. I wrote up a list and left most of my stuff to Alice, since she was a girl and all I had was two school dresses with patches and the party dress Lexie got me, which didn't fit no more 'cause I growed too tall. And I had me a doll MeeMaw made me, stayed on my bed, that didn't look like a doll no more 'cause it was a rag doll and lived up to isself through the years 'cause I dragged it everywhere I went when I was a little kid. I had three marbles; one was a cat's eye, real pretty, so I left them to Irl, 'case he lived and I prayed he'd make it even if I didn't. I left Mama the quilt MeeMaw made for my bed and I left a note for Melvin and Lexie telling them why I didn't leave them nothing; there weren't nothing left to leave, but I put a P.S. on the end of the note to tell them what I would of left them if I could of bought something to leave 'em. For Melvin, I said I'd leave him some of the white gravel stones from our trailer lot if we had us a trailer, so's his lot would look better, and for Lexie, I said I'd leave some seeds from our flower beds if we had a flower bed round the trailer, if we had a trailer, so she'd have pretty flowers round her trailer. And for Mama I left another

P.S. giving her all the money in the jars, 'case the March of Dimers and Penniers never come. Then I was ready, even though I didn't want to go.

Two more weeks come and gone. When I didn't die I tore up that list and figured the batch they sent us musta been all right after all, which was a relief 'cause my birthday was coming and I didn't want to miss it. I'd be ten. Mz. Pence said all birthdays is special, but ten was extra special, so I sure didn't want to miss that one. Carolee missed hers by only one year and that always made me feel bad, so I was planning to share mine with her at her grave spot. John Benjamin and me was making up the birthday plans already. We was fixin' to surprise her with a really nice party. I even saved two pennies out of the March of Pennies jar to get balloons; one for Carolee and one for me. I sure hoped they wouldn't mind me holding out two pennies to pay for them. I put a note in the jar explaining how Carolee died so sad like, and how she missed out on her tenth birthday and all, so's they'd know why them two pennies I first 'tended to give 'em was missing.

Little Irl was still in that iron lung machine that breathed for him. Sounded like a terrible thing, a machine that breathed your lungs. I hoped it didn't hurt him none. He was only two years and a handful of months old. But that was only the half of it. That polio crippled children. It shaped their bodies like it wanted to, instead of how God intended to. Made it so they couldn't walk, maybe never again even. Some had metal braces on their legs to help 'em walk. And some got put in wheelchairs. It was real sorrowful. People all over was getting it. Trudy Anne's little brother Edgar died 'fore they knew he even had it, and a boy at school, Gordon Paddy, got crippled by it. He come back to school with braces on both his legs. He had to have this therapy every day to stretch his legs, and he said he screamed something awful 'cause it hurt so bad.

"Gettin' crippled must have made you stupid," Darla Faye said. "I'd never let them do that to me."

"I got no choice, Darla Faye," he said. "My legs will stiffin up and never bend again if'n I don't stretch 'em out every day," Gordon told her. He dragged hisself across the playground. Them crutches he used looked like they might hurt a body's underarm parts to me.

"I think he's real brave, Darla Faye," I said.

"Oh, what do you know anyway, Lori Jean?" she said.

"My uncle Melvin said it takes a whole lot of courage to git through polio."

"What's he know?"

"Well, his little boy Irl done got polio and they got him over in Grady Hospital in one a' them iron lungs. He said Irl's the bravest little fella he knows. That's what he said."

"Well, my daddy said your uncle Melvin and your step-daddy come from bad stock. He said they'll never 'mount to nothin'."

"Well, I don't think your daddy rightly knows for sure somebody's future," I said.

"He's a good judge a' people, Lori Jean," she said. "That's why he's the boss man." Darla Faye smiled her make-believe smile and smoothed the ruffles on her dress. It was the one I liked the best; the blue one with white dots. She wore a different one every day of the week. I watched her run on over to play tetherball with Trudy Anne. I sure hoped she was wrong about what she said. Nothing against her daddy; Noble Brewster was the boss man, but that didn't give him the right to judge people. MeeMaw said that was the Lord's job. Noble Brewster's was to mind the mill.

Ray was still at Grady Hospital in the burn place. He was

getting a bit better every day. Uncle Melvin, he made a deal with Mr. Jenkins and got us one of his old trailers! Worked at night fixing it up and we moved in. Mama and me helped a bunch. Things was looking up. We was was praying at church and in between times, too, that God made the fire to make a new man out of him. We was praying for Little Irl, too.

"Please, God," I said, "let Little Irl get outa that iron breathin' machine. He's a real nice little kid, he is, no trouble a'tall. And Alice, she's real sorrowful without him. And please, Lord, don't let his legs get stuck in them braces. He's a little fella likes to jump and climb more than any little fella I knowed." I was hoping he'd answer. I reminded him they was twins and didn't like being without the other much, which were the truth. Alice was looking all over for Irl and fretting herself something terrible. Not even a cookie helped. Mostly she just dragged her blanket round the trailer looking behind doors and under the bed like Irl was playing hide-and-seek on her and forgot to tell her. It broke off another piece of my heart just watching Alice. Her little legs toddled all over that trailer searching for Irl. And him not even there. He was still in that iron lung, not getting any better a'tall. Melvin come home from the hospital that night with even worse news. I heard his truck pull up on them gravel stones right next to our gravel stones keeped us from getting stuck in the mud when it rained. Melvin's stepladder was in the back. He and Lexie used it to climb up and see Irl from outside his window, 'cause he was quarantined and nobody could touch him, 'cepting the nurses and they had to wear themselves these special clothes to do it. They looked mighty peculiar, dressed in them long white covers. They even wore masks and they had gloves on their hands like that Dracula fella Chester Britt had a picture of, he showed me once. Them nurses was right nice, but still, they probably scared Little Irl real good first time he seen them. Imagine being in a strange place without your mama, with them critters roaming the halls, got masks and gloves and pointed caps on their heads; had me worried plenty Little Irl wouldn't sleep good, 'cause he didn't like scary things. And in particular he didn't like ghosts. And for sure Alice didn't. They run for cover when Ray pretended he was one on Halloween and stuck an old sheet over his head and cut eyeball holes so's he could see.

"Boooooooo," Ray yelled in a voice so deep made me jump. He come right out of the bushes at us, right when I was fixing to take Little Irl and Alice trick-or-treating for their very first time. They went toddling back up the steps and into the house as fast as their chubby little legs could carry them, howling for Lexie. Mama come out and seen Ray was laughing like one a' them hyena dogs so ugly.

"What's goin' on?" When I told her, she laid into Ray good.

"That's not funny, Ray, and you know it!" she said. "You want to scar them childrens for life? Take that silly sheet off and behave yourself." Sometimes my mama sure was brave, but usually not. She hardly never crossed Ray. Maybe once in a blue moon if he was hurting some young'uns or something. Mostly she knew better. Ray's likely to kill you soon's look at you if he's in the mood to and you cross him. I never got to take Irl and Alice trick-or-treating that night after all. They wouldn't come out of the house and wouldn't even come to the door when Lexie give out candy to all the other kids. They hid behind the curtain, they's so scared. It was right before the next Halloween that Irl got sick, so there he was in an iron lung machine, and he hadn't even been trick-or-treating. That weren't right a'tall. I planned on making sure the next one coming up would be different for them. Seems the least I could do, seeing as it was my stepdaddy ruined it for them the year before.

If Irl was afraid of them nurses at first, he got over it. Uncle Melvin said he was a favorite of theirs, and they spoiled him best they could, all things considered. That night Melvin pulled his truck up on the gravel, I looked out the window and when I seen Lexie wasn't with him I went running to the door.

"Uncle Melvin," I yelled, "where's Lexie? Is she all right?" Mama come out on the step. Melvin got out of his truck and headed for our door. His face was the color of meat sat too long and spoiled.

"What's goin' on, Melvin?" Mama said. "You don't look too good. Where's Lexie?" My stomach decided it was a yo-yo and tried to make me sick. It flopped up and down inside me, and a bad taste come up in my throat. I swallowed hard to wash it back down, but it ended up tasting even worse.

"Uncle Melvin . . . Uncle Melvin . . . ," I said, half crying. "What's wrong? Where's Lexie?"

"Lexie's fine. Mz. Hawkins is bringing her home, but the doctors don't think Irl's gonna make it." Melvin's shoulders slumped forward. For a minute I thought he was gonna fall. Mama grabbed a hold of his arm.

"Oh, Melvin, I'm so sorry," she said. "Come on in. You don't need to be alone with this." Mama held the door open and Melvin went in. Me and Mama followed.

"I don't want Lexie to know. She might have the baby too soon," he said. Melvin gathered Mama under one arm and me under the other.

"Uncle Melvin," I said, "are you sure? Ain't there nothin' them doctors kin do?"

"They're doin' everything they can, Lori Jean, everything they . . ." Uncle Melvin couldn't talk no more. He buried his face into my mama's long hair. His shoulders started heaving and his arms was squeezing us so hard together in a circle we was like one person.

I didn't want to think about Little Irl dying. I didn't want to think about our going on without him, but with all the crying and carrying on there was no getting around it. I remembered what MeeMaw always said about birthing and dying.

"When you were born, Lori Jean," she said, "you were cryin' and everyone round you was smilin'. Live your life, honey," MeeMaw said, "so when you die, you'll be smilin' and everyone round you will be cryin'."

Here Little Irl wasn't quite three years old and already he lived his life so everyone around him was crying.

"Uncle Melvin?" I said. "When you seen Little Irl tonight, was he smilin'? Was he?"

"Yep, he sure enough was, Lori Jean," he said. "Lexie read him that storybook you bought for him." I thought about Lexie climbing up that ladder with her belly sticking out, her face all pressed against the window screen, trying to get a look-see at Little Irl.

"Yep, he was smilin' real good when I left," Melvin said.

"Seems only right," I said, "him being such a fine little fellow and all."

"Smiling?" Mama said. "What in the dickens are you talking about, Lori Jean? Little fella's dying!" So I told them what MeeMaw told me about birthing and dying. We hugged each other good and cried 'til we couldn't no more 'cause Lexie was gonna be back any minute. Mama said to dry our eyes and pretend everything was fine. And that was a real hard thing to pretend. When Lexie come through the door, Mama and Melvin fooled her good. When I looked in both their eyes, I couldn't even tell nothin' was wrong, and here I knew there was. But I wasn't sure mine could fool Lexie none, so I rubbed my eyes to cover them good.

"I sure am tired, Mama," I said. "Kin I git on your bed and rest myself for a spell whilst y'all visit?"

"Sure, honey," Mama said. They each give me a hug, but I didn't hug 'em back too good. I just keeped rubbing at my eyes, pretending I was too tired to see straight. I done a good job, too. I walked right into the wall. Got me another goose egg; showed up come morning.

chapter sixteen

"Now don't be starin' at his face when he gets here, Lori Jean," Mama said.

"I'll just look good when he ain't lookin' back," I said.

"Lori Jean!"

"Well, I ain't never seen a body scarred up from no burns a'fore," I said. "I reckon it'll be all right, long as he don't see me."

Uncle Melvin was bringing Ray home from the burn place at Grady Hospital. I sure hoped he didn't look like a patchwork quilt 'cause he weren't none too pretty to start with, what with his daddy beating his face all in when he was a boy. And I sure hoped he wouldn't pester me about that sack full of money 'cause then I'd have to lie about it again. MeeMaw always said she could spot a liar from twenty feet with one eye closed. Maybe Ray could, too, now that he was pretty much all better.

I didn't like telling no lie, even if it was to make things right. I just prayed he'd forgotten all about it. Ray only asked me about that money sack one time in the hospital when he was coming round from all them drugs they give him. It was the only time they let me in to see him. First Mama and Lexie went to see about getting in to see Irl down on the children's floor. We didn't have no ladder with us and Mama wanted to ask if there was any way Lexie could poke her head in, talk to Little Irl while we sat with Ray.

"You keep Ray company, Lori Jean. We'll be back 'fore long," Mama said.

"Can't I come poke my head in, too?"

"They don't let children on that floor 'less you're there yourself, Lori Jean," she said. "You're right lucky they're letting you in to see your stepdaddy, honey, don't ya' think?"

"Pretty lucky," I said. I stayed with Ray while they went on down to the little children's ward. Ray was laying in a metal bed had a crank at the bottom.

"How are ya' feeling, Ray?" I asked. "Are they taking good care of ya'?" I went and stood next to him at the side of the bed. His face was bandaged up where only one eye stuck out. He looked like one a' them mummies Mz. Pence showed us, except Ray was alive and the ones she showed us was dead.

"How the hell do you think I feel?" he said.

"I was hopin' you might be feelin' a bit better."

"Well, I ain't."

"Little Irl, he's real sick," I said. "Mama and me's prayin' . . ."

"Where's that sack I had in my hand?"

"Want me to crank your bed up some . . . ?"

"That sack I had in my hand, day a' the fire, where is it?"

"Don't you remember, Ray?" I said. "That bag got burned up in the fire. It was right there on the kitchen floor. Burned clean up, 'member?"

"The whole damn thing burned?" he said.

"Uh-huh . . . ," I said. I couldn't tell if he were relieved it was gone and he was safe from being put in the jailhouse or if he were just real sorrowful he couldn't somehow go git it. Them bandages all over his head kept me from reading his face like I used to could.

"Yep, it sure enough burned," I lied that day. "But it was a nasty old bag, Ray," I said. "Burned clean up." He didn't ask me no more questions about it that day, so I sure hoped that he wouldn't now he was home.

Maybe some of his brains got too close to the fire and got a bit burned on the edges. They might coulda and then maybe he'd never remember nothing. I'd find out soon enough.

Uncle Melvin was pulling up next to our trailer that very minute. Mama was looking out the window and fussing with her hair. She even had her go-to-church dress on.

"He's here, Lori Jean!" Mama said. "Be nice now."

"I will, Mama," I said, and I planned to. We could get us a whole new start. Ray was gonna work for Mr. Jenkins real soon to pay on this trailer they fixed up for us and the rest of the money was gonna be for us to get ahead, Mama said. She was gonna keep working for Mz. Hawkins, too. We was gonna get us a passel of money. Ray didn't need to steal hisself no money. We'd have ourselves plenty of honest money we earned ourselves. That's the only kind to have, else ya' can't sleep good at night and ya' can't get to heaven, neither.

"Hi, hon," Mama said when Ray come through the door. "Let me help ya'." She took hold of his arm and he followed her to the sofa.

"I fixed a nice lunch for ya', and Lori Jean put clean sheets on the bed, 'case you want to take a nap."

"Welcome home, Ray," I said. "Ain't this trailer something?" He looked around a bit.

"Guess it'll do."

"It was right nice a' everybody to help us out after the fire, don't ya' think, Ray?" I said. "Folks come from all over, brought food and stuff. Melvin and Mr. Jenkins set up the trailer. . . ."

"You don't need to remind me none, girl, what I owes to everybody. I just got home," Ray said.

"What Lori Jean's tryin' to say is . . ."

"She's tryin' to rub it in, me not bein' able to provide none," Ray said before Mama run over and plumped a pillow up behind his head.

"Here, hon, you just relax and I'm gonna bring you a nice plate a' cold fried chicken, just the way ya' like it." Ray laid down and shut his eyes. I decided I best not talk to him none. He was twisting my words into something they wasn't.

"Thanks for bringin' him home, Melvin," Mama said. "You want some chicken 'fore you go?"

"No thanks, Nadine. I want to check on Lexie. I ain't told her yet what the doctor said about Irl."

"Oh, Melvin," Mama said. "Are you sure you should? You don't want her goin' into labor too early, now."

"I wouldn't tell her a'tall, but there's a good chance she'll overhear the nurses at the hospital talkin'. . . ."

"Even so, Melvin, you best wait. Speak to them nurses yourself. Tell 'em to hush when Lexie's around visitin'. They'll understand."

"I don't know. . . . ," Melvin said. "Lori Jean, can you take care a' little Alice while we head on over to the hospital?"

"Sure I kin, Uncle Melvin."

"You eat somethin' first, Lori Jean. You're too thin. You don't eat enough to keep a bird goin'," Mama said.

"I'll just take me one a' these drumsticks, Mama," I said, "and a biscuit. That's plenty 'til supper." I wrapped it up in some plain butcher paper and headed next door. I liked taking care of Alice. She was learning new words every day and hardly never stopped talking.

Lexie was making some mashed potatoes when I got there.

"Hi, Aunt Lexie," I said. "I can finish that for ya' so ya'll can get goin'."

"Look who's here, Alice. It's Lori Jean," Lexie said. Alice banged on her high chair with her spoon and sent a handful of Cheerios flying in all directions. She thought it was so funny she kept it up 'til Lexie took the spoon away from her. Alice let out a howl.

"This is for your mashed potatoes, sugar," Lexie said. "You kin have it back when they're ready. Now hush."

"I'll finish 'em," I said.

"Thank you, Lori Jean," Lexie said. "We'll be back in a few hours. You go get your mama if you need some help," Lexie said.

"I will."

"She'll be ready for her nap in a bit. She's been up since seven."

"I'll read her a story when she finishes her 'taters and put her down," I said. "Tell Little Irl one a' them kisses you blow is from me, 'kay?" I said. "I sure do miss havin' him around."

"I know," Lexie said. "We all do, but he'll be home soon; I gota feelin'." Lexie wrapped a sweater around her shoulders. It was way too small for her now that her belly stuck out so far. "And what with this new baby fixin' to get here soon," Lexie said, patting her tummy, "we'll be knee-deep in young'uns agin."

"Oh, that'll be nice," I said and give her a smile. I sure hoped she couldn't tell what I was thinking. Uncle Melvin said the doctors was still pretty sure Little Irl wouldn't make it. I prayed he'd hang on 'til after the new baby got here.

"Dear God," I said, "if you're sendin' one of your angels down to pick up Little Irl, could you send the slowest one you got?" I explained how babies had to be in their mamas for a proper spell 'fore they's ready and how Lexie's baby weren't likely ready.

"Lexie ain't supposed to have that baby too soon," I said. "And for sure she probably will, if one a' yore angels shows up."

Uncle Melvin and Lexie weren't gone very long. Lexie wasn't feeling real good. She was having some pains in her back and decided she best come home and rest. Mama come over and fixed Uncle Melvin and Alice supper and I went home to stay with Ray. He took hisself a good nap and seemed to be in much better spirits.

"You want to play some gin rummy, Ray?" I asked him. "That's a good way to pass the time, don't ya' think?" We played ourselves some gin rummy and I made sure Ray won most hands so he wouldn't get mad or nothing, but I won one ever' now and then so he wouldn't catch on to me.

"Lori Jean, where's that flour sack you said burned up in the fire?" he said. That's what I was afraid would happen.

"It burned up, Ray," I said. "You know that."

"Well now, if that sack burned up, how come me and you didn't burn up with it?"

"Well, you was plenty burned up, Ray, and I got sorta burned up," I said. "That old sack just burned up quicker is all. Gin!" I laid my hand of cards down, hoping to git his mind back on the game. He counted up the points and wrote 'em down.

"And how come you never asked me what's so important about that sack I keep askin' you about?" That were a really good question, and I hadn't thought on that one a'fore and I surely should have 'cause now I didn't have me no good answer to give him.

"Well," I said, "I guess I was plumb eat up with how you was doin' and whether you'd get better, so I wasn't thinkin' straight. But now you're pretty much well, so how come it is you're always askin' about that old sack?" I said, pretending like I didn't much care, but for truth, my heart was pounding in my chest like it were a drum and my breathing was going in and out my nose to beat all Dixie.

"Had some papers in it I need. Stuff for our future."

"Well," I said, "we best git on with the future we got 'cause that old sack just burned all up."

Ray stared me down real good.

"You best not be lyin', girl," he said.

"I ain't lying, Ray. MeeMaw didn't raise me to tell no lies." I sure hoped to heaven I wasn't going to hell 'cause now I done lied about lying.

Mama come home then and told me to go on to bed. She unfolded the cot for me and put my bedcovers down. Ray moved from the sofa on into their bedroom. I heard them getting ready for bed.

"Tomorrow I'm goin' out there."

"Be a waste a' time. There ain't nothin' left," Mama said. "It burnt to the ground, Ray."

"Just wanna mosey around."

"There ain't nothin' to see," Mama said.

"Got nothin' better to do. Doc says I can't work for at least a week."

"Suit yourself."

Ray was going out to our old place. He thought I was lying for sure. He was gonna search on that flour sack. I just had to get that money back to the mill, but there was no way I could do it 'fore morning. I didn't sleep none too good that night worrying on it. I had this dream where the sheriff come and took my mama away. Said she stole the payroll. In the dream Ray was all burned up and laying on the ground when they come for her. And I was laying right next to him. Carolee was there, too, and she was putting flowers in my hair. Every time she tucked a flower in, Ray sat up and pulled it out and threw it into Roseflower Creek. When Carolee run out of flowers, he laid back down on the ground, closed his eyes, and I got up and walked off.

I think it was probably the strangest dream I ever had, but most a' the time I forget my dreams soon's I wake up, so I couldn't be sure. I got up to git me a drink of water, then laid back down on the cot trying to sleep. When morning come, that dream was still fresh on my mind. I didn't understand it none. Mostly, I never understood my dreams much. They was always mixed-up stuff, but this one scared me good. I keeped seeing my mama dragged off in the squad car and me walking the other way and all the while Ray dead on the ground.

He was gone by the time I woke up in the morning. Mama was out feeding the chickens.

"Mama." I stood in the doorway and called to her. "You forgot to get me up to help you 'fore school."

"I heard you tossin' and turnin' all night. I figured you best sleep in a bit," she said.

"I had me one a' them nightmares," I said. Mama finished up and come in the trailer.

"I'll fix you breakfast and you kin tell me all about it."

"Mostly I can't remember it much," I said. I sure didn't want to tell her about no payroll money and her being taken away and Ray dead and me just walking away.

"Where's Ray?" I asked. 'Course I already knew, but it was a good way not to talk about my dream.

"He went on over to our old place. Seems to think he might find some a' our stuff."

"I might should go help him. Make sure he don't hurt hisself none, just gettin' out a' the hospital and all," I said.

"Why, Lori Jean, you got school. You can't be caterin' to that man's foolishness."

"I could miss me one day a' school. Mz. Pence would understand."

"No need for that. I suspect he'll be back soon, once he sees there ain't nothin' left." Mama fixed me some grits and a cold biscuit left over from supper.

"You want I should heat this up for ya'?"

"No, ma'am," I said. "But some butter and some a' MeeMaw's marmalade would be right nice." I rather fancied cold biscuits with fresh butter and marmalade. Kinda like having dessert for breakfast.

I was hoping Ray would come back 'fore I left for school, so I could see how he acted and find out if he found anything. I dallied 'til I couldn't no more without bein' late, but he didn't make it home 'fore I left. It made for a long school day. Twice Mz. Pence called on me and I wasn't listening.

"Lori Jean, am I boring you?" she asked me the second time she seen I wasn't paying attention.

"Oh, no ma'am," I said. "Everything's real interestin', it sure enough is," I said and nodded my head. "I guess my noggin just don't realize it yet." The class thought that was funny and started laughing. Mz. Pence called everybody to order, then decided we might as well take recess and refresh ourselves.

I had me a real bad feeling in my stomach on the way home from school. I never been on one a' them roller coasters like the one Carolee's cousin Eugenia went on at a place called Coney Island one summer. Eugenia said it flipped her tummy up and down 'til it felt like it would fall right out of her bottom. She said they stood in line over and over and rode it again and again 'fore the day was over and had themselves a real fun time. My stomach was heaving up and down like that and it surely wasn't fun. Why would anyone stand in line and pay good money to have their stomach flipped up and down and all about like that? Why, that's crazy. By the time I got to the trailer my innards was about sick to death worrying about what Ray might of found. I opened the door and he was sitting there on the sofa waiting on me. His eyes was mean as a bat got the rabies and they was aimed at mine; two pointed daggers fixin' to blind me. It give me a worse case of the shivers than taking a bath when we run out of hot water.

"Lori Jean!" he said. My name come up out of the back part of his throat like a growl. He was a mad dog, gonna bite me; tear me apart. I tried to run before he could sink his teeth in, but it was too late. 'Fore I knew it, he had me. He sunk his claws deep into my arm.

chapter seventeen

"Found this, Lori Jean," Ray said. He held up a piece of the flour sack.

"Where'd you find that?" I asked, knowing full well he must of pulled it from the edge of the outhouse.

"It was layin' on the ground, stuck in a board that was once our front stoop," he said. My stomach finally stopped flippin'. I was sorely relieved.

"If it was that close to the door, why in thunder didn't you yank the whole damn sack out in the yard for chrissake?"

"Ray, we was burnin' all up! I had fire on my back and yore hands was meltin'. I did me the best I could." Mama come out of the bedroom.

"What's goin' on?" she asked us.

"Nothin'," I said.

"What's this 'bout a flour sack got burned in the fire?"

"Just a sack with some papers in it's all," Ray said.

"What kind a' papers?"

"Shoot, just papers on the truck, the deed to yore ma's house, just some stuff," he said.

"I got the deed for Mama's house right in the bureau

drawer," she said. "Won't do us no good. It weren't insured."

"Well then, we don't gotta worry 'bout no papers burned up in the fire. We be done with it," Ray said. He give me a dirty look and got up off the sofa and walked outside. I sure hoped we was done with it. We would be, too, if I could get that money back to the mill. That was the only problem I had in the whole world. That and Little Irl being so sick. Everything else was going right good for us.

In fact, having our trailer parked next to Lexie and Melvin's worked out mighty fine. At night Mama and Lexie and I got down on our knees and prayed for God to heal Little Irl and bring him back home to us. But poor little Alice, she was fretting all the time, not having her brother there with her. We all missed him a bunch. He was a real special little rascal, he was. I would of rather me got the polio than him, but Mama said that's not how it works.

"We don't get to choose our crosses, Lori Jean," she told me.

"Well, that's real sorrowful, Mama," I said, "'cause here I've had me near ten whole years and Little Irl he ain't even had hisself three. Don't seem right."

"There ain't no wrong or right to it, Lori Jean. That's the way it is. You just gotta accept it is all," she said.

"Well, I'm not gonna," I said. "I'm not gonna and that's that."

'Course there wasn't much I could do, so I just prayed some more for one a' them miracles. And I drew Irl more of them little pictures of trains and boats he liked so much. The trains was his favorite. And I even read him a story one time. I had to climb Melvin's ladder and stand on my tippy toes outside the hospital window to do it. It was his favorite book in the whole world; a picture story 'bout a little train that thinks he can't, 'til he finds out that he can. I bought it with some of the money Mz. Hawkins give me for helping out. Irl liked it real fine and he never got tired of it, no matter how many times we read it to him. Uncle Melvin and Aunt Lexie usually done the reading, but that one day I got to.

"Climb on up there, Lori Jean," Uncle Melvin said. "Stand real still when you turn them pages, now. I got your legs," he said. It was a pretty short book, but even so, it took me a while to read 'cause I wanted Irl to see the pretty pictures, best he could, so I turned them around and held them against the screen before I went on to the next page. Them hospital folks had him in this isolation place called a ward. I'm not sure how good Irl seen them pictures through that mesh, and I keeped thinking his neck must been sore having to turn it toward the window all that time, but if it were he didn't fuss none about it.

"Read me agin," he said, and I did, and two times more after that even. But then my legs, right below the backs of my knees, cramped me so bad I had to reach down and rub them and I dropped the book. Uncle Melvin handed it back up to me, but them cramps got to hurting me something awful. I rubbed at them again; all the while Irl begged me to read some more.

"Agin! Agin!" he said. But I couldn't. The pain was worse than a pack of wolves having my calves for their dinner. I tried to be brave like Little Irl and not pay the hurting no mind, but I didn't do a good job of it. Tears was gathering in the corners of my eyes, fixing to be a river I couldn't stop, like the ones flowed all them times Ray whipped me with his big-buckled strap. I surly didn't want Little Irl to see me bawling, feeling sorry for myself when he been so brave over all his suffering. No sirree. I needed to get me down off that ladder lickety-split before I started howling like a baby got a bad diaper rash.

"I'm sorry, Little Irl," I said. "I'd sure like to, but my legs ain't gonna let me. They's tighter than a rubber band been stretched too far. Maybe I kin come back tomorrow after school, okay?"

"Okeedokee, okeedokee . . . ," he said. Isn't he something? He didn't complain or nothing. I blew him a kiss as best I could through that metal screen and barely made it down the ladder steps 'fore I started shrieking. I wanted to be brave, but I was a coward for sure.

"Uncle Melvin!" I said. "I got me these powerful aches in my legs. I think I done caught the polio!" I jumped around in a circle like a chicken got his head cut off and don't know it yet.

"You got one a' them charley horses, Lori Jean," Uncle Melvin said, "from standing on your toes so long. Let me help ya'."

"You sure it ain't the polio, Uncle Melvin?" I cried. "It hurts bad, reeeeaaal bad!"

"It's a charley horse, sweet thang," he said. He set me on the ground and started to rub the back of one a' my legs that had a knot big as his fist in it.

"Yep. It's a charley horse, all right. Had me plenty a' them," he said.

"They's two a' them, Uncle Melvin," I said. "And if they's horses, they thinks they's wolves. They sure enough do."

"Here, let me rub the other one, too," Uncle Melvin said. "Have you fixed up in no time." Like always, he was right. Them horses took off for parts unknown, just like he said they would. But they come back once in a while, usually in the middle of the night, and I jumped me out of bed and stomped up and down, howling like I's the wolf. Then I rubbed them good like Uncle Melvin showed me and they took off for wherever it was cramps come from. Fancy that! They always hurt me a bunch before they leaved, but I tried to think on what MeeMaw always said.

"Everything's a blessing, Lori Jean. You remember that. All things work for the glory of God, so praise His name in all things, ya' hear?" she said, or something like that, best I recall. So I'm glad I got me them charley things that day at Grady Hospital while I was standing on that stepladder too long. If I wouldn't a' got me them charley pains that day, whilst I read that story over and over to Little Irl, then I wouldn't a' knowed what to do with 'em when they come at me in the middle of the night, when there weren't no one close by to help me. So MeeMaw was right. Everything's a blessing, I guess. Exceptin', I couldn't see how Irl's polio was a blessing. That part had me real confused. I figured MeeMaw could of explained it, but it was beyond me. When I asked Mama, she didn't have no answer. She said she wished she did. And I couldn't hardly ask Uncle Melvin and Aunt Lexie how it was a blessing for Little Irl to suffer. Didn't seem right. So I put that question in my heart in a spot with all the others I'd saved up. I planned on asking Jesus for the answers once I growed old and died and went to heaven like MeeMaw.

All them months Lexie grew the new baby in her tummy, we watched Little Irl get worse. It hurt so bad to see him stuck in that iron lung machine. It got so I hated looking through that mesh window when I climbed the stepladder every Sunday after church. Mama'd climb up first, then Uncle Melvin, and then me. Aunt Lexie couldn't climb it much in the end. Her belly got too big and Melvin was sore afraid she'd fall. She'd stand below the window and yell out, "It's Mama, sugar! Can you hear me, honey?"

"Mama . . . Mama . . . ," Little Irl called back that first time Uncle Melvin wouldn't let Lexie up the ladder no more.

"See me! See me!" Little Irl said. "Climb up, Mama, see me!"

"I can't, baby," Lexie said. Her voice cracked. "But I will, honey, soon's this new little brother or sister you got comin' gets here, okay?" she yelled. "Mama loves you, punkin. Be brave, okay?"

"Okeedokee . . . ," Irl said, no crying or complaining. He was a special one, I'm telling ya'. That day when I watched Lexie call out to Little Irl, knowing they couldn't hold each other like mamas and little childrens is supposed to, and knowing how much Lexie loved hugging and kissing on her childrens every chance she got, some more pieces of my heart got broke off.

"How many parts can I lose . . . ," I asked God, "and still have me one left?" He must of thought I was funning—and I wasn't—'cause he didn't answer. Then a' one them miracles happened. Irl, he started getting better. The doctors said they couldn't rightly explain it. Somes got better, somes didn't, and somes died.

So we had ourselves some really good news what with Irl getting better. It wasn't long after that the doctors let Uncle Melvin and Aunt Lexie bring him home from the hospital. What a day that was. First we all got down on our knees and thanked God for the miracle he give us. Even Ray. Exceptin' he didn't move his lips with the rest of us when we said the big prayer named after the Lord, but still he kept on his knees all the while we prayed it, so I figured it counted. Then we had ourselves one fine party with store-bought cookies and Coca-Cola even. And the days that followed kept getting better. I was mighty happy, I'm telling ya'. Nothing wrong with that. I figured God wants us all to be happy or why'd he make us? Even so, I should of knowed to be prepared for when the bad days come, 'cause MeeMaw showed me in the Bible once where it's promised we get a equal share of each, but I forgot about that part. Made the days to come even tougher to take, not being prepared and all. MeeMaw said the bad times was to make us kinder people.

"Suffering does a heap bit a' good, child," she said. "Makes us privy to the pain of others. Helps us appreciate all the good the Lord sends our way, 'cause then we got something to compare it to. Always remember, Lori Jean, when it's over, we're better people for it." And I believed her. All the same, it was hard to take when the bad come calling, especially the way it chose to do it.

I was helping Lexie with the twins after school. She was fixing to have the new baby any day and her belly was popped out front like a watermelon shoulda already burst.

"Doc Crawley says it's gonna be a big'un," she told Uncle Melvin. "Honey, I jist don't think I can take the pain again."

"Now, sugar, the second time is gonna be a whole lot easier. Don't you fret none, ya' hear?" he told her. She was still pretty much having herself a hissy fit each day it got closer. It was pretty much getting me upset, too. All that blood and screaming last time.

"What's it like havin' babies, Mama?" I asked that night after supper when we was washing up the dishes. We was having one of them girl talks, getting closer all the time. I was almost ten. Ray was sitting out on the steps leading up to the trailer, acting real strange, all peaceful like, which weren't like him a'tall. Hadn't had a drop a liquor we knowed of in a month of Sundays. He was like Chester Britt's yo-yo, he was. 'Cepting Melvin said this time Ray's being sober might could be permanent on account he near died in the fire.

"Did ya' hear me, Mama?" She was lost in her daydreams, I guess, and didn't answer.

"What?"

"That pain ladies have when they's havin' babies, what's it like?"

"No sense frettin' yourself over that none, Lori Jean. It'll come soon enough, I reckon."

"I'm not frettin', Mama. I jist want ta' understand is all. How come it hurts so much? And why can't them doctors give Lexie somethin' so she won't have to suffer so bad?"

" 'Cause there just ain't nothin' strong enough to kill that kinda pain, Lori Jean, and there never will be. It's in the Bible. It's our punishment for Eve givin' Adam that apple to eat when the Lord done told her not to."

"But Mama, that ain't fair. Lexie wouldn't give nobody a apple they wasn't s'posed to have, nohow," I said.

"Well, life ain't fair, Lori Jean. It's spelled L-I-F-E. If'n it were fair, it'd be F-A-I-R. You best git used to it," she said. I guess there weren't no arguing that. Lexie was on her own.

The very next morning it happened. It was still dark when Uncle Melvin dropped the twins off at our place and hauled Lexie off in the Chevy to the hospital clear over in Decatur. I ran outside in my nightie to tell Lexie I'd be praying for a miracle, so's God would forgive Eve what she done, but they was clear down the dirt road 'fore I could.

"Lori Jean," Mama called out, "git back inside 'fore you catch a shiver." It was right cold that winter morning at that. March 12. I remember 'cause late the next night Melvin and Lexie had themselves a baby girl on March 13. It was a Friday and Mama said it was bad luck; that the baby was born with a cloud over her head for sure and only bad things would happen to her. They named her Iris Anne. She weighed eight pounds and had black hair like Melvin and a whole lot of it, too. It took Lexie near two days trying to get that baby out and after all that she had herself one of them cereal sections where they cut her belly open. Her and little Iris near died. It's the only time I recall ever hearing Melvin curse.

"Why in the hell them jackass doctors couldn't a' done that golldang operation to begin with instead a' puttin' her through all that sufferin' is beyond me," Melvin said. He was fit to be tied. "I oughta kick ass and take names a' them sons-a-bitchers," he said.

Later he found out why they waited so long and then he really started cursing, and I ain't gonna repeat them words he said nohow, being so close to heaven and all. The reason was they wanted ta' make sure he had hisself the right kind a' assurance or something from the cotton mill so's it would pay the bill. It cost over one hundred dollars! Seems rich folks git that operation 'fore they pay, but poor folks gotta pay first. In the end Melvin said the only reason they done the operation at all was to save her life.

"Lexie was dyin'," he said, "and they figured the baby might, too, so's they had no choice. Otherwise they woulda left her sufferin' 'til she got that young'un out on her own, them sons-a-bitchers." Those are his own words 'cause I'm not trying to swear me no words. He was so mad I'm telling ya'. It was really something and I don't rightly blame him none. Seems like the right thing to do would be treat everybody the same.

Uncle Melvin was fretting all that week about the hospital wanting their money and the doctors pestering him about filing some papers so's they could get paid. Mama was having a time of it, too. She was fretting herself over all the doctor and hospital bills stacking up from Ray's time in the burn unit at Grady. She tried to keep 'em from Ray. I think she was afraid he'd start drinking again if he seen how many there was. I heard her and Uncle Melvin talking about going down to the business office together and setting up payments or something.

"Trouble is, Melvin," Mama said, "there ain't a penny extra for payments. What am I gonna do?"

It was the first time I seen Melvin didn't have no answers. He just shook his head like he didn't know, and here he always knowed just about everything.

I could of given my dimes and pennies, but the March of Dimers come weeks ago and got 'em. Melvin didn't have any money to spare, and he was having trouble getting the insurance people to pay what they was supposed to. That's when they took Lexie from this nice room they give her, called her a indigent or something, and put her in another room with twenty-some other ladies. I don't rightly understand it all even now, but it made Melvin's face turn red and his breathing come out funny.

I coulda told them Melvin was good for paying what he owed. He was the most honest, hard-working man I knowed, but it didn't seem to make no difference to them 'cause Melvin was complaining over and over about how they wouldn't listen and take Lexie back to her regular room where he wanted her. Mama said he was plumb eat up with regret that he didn't have the money to do right by Lexie.

"Lori Jean, men's ability to take care a' their loved ones is all tied up with their manness. If'n they can't do one, they can't do the other." I didn't rightly understand all that none, but Mama knew a whole lotta things now. MeeMaw said that would happen.

"It's called wisdom, Lori Jean," she said. "You git it by makin' a whole lotta mistakes and remembering them." So my mama was right smart by then 'cause she'd made herself a whole lotta mistakes. Truth be known, Ray was prob'ly her biggest.

After they took Lexie over to that room with all them other ladies scrunched together, Melvin seemed like a changed man. Plumb angry, he was. Always talking about us and them, and whoever "them" was, he didn't like 'em much a'tall. He'd go see Lexie and the baby every day when he finished at the mill before he'd go over to Mr. Jenkins's trailer lot. Then, when he got done working there, he'd come over to our place to pick up the twins. I always helped carry Alice back to her bed and he took Irl. Then he'd fix me a cold glass of lemonade as a "thank yee" treat.

It was my favorite time of the day, now Carolee was gone. Uncle Melvin and me, we'd sit and talk and he'd pour hisself a glass of whiskey. He never been one to drink much, but he was doing a bit of it lately, I noticed. But he didn't get mean or nothing like Ray did when he drunk. Fancy that! Ray was sober now and sound asleep next door, fixing to go to work in the morning and Melvin was pouring hisself a whiskey. Life sure had a way of turning tables. MeeMaw always said ya' can't never count on things staying the same.

"Don't takes nothing for granted, Lori Jean," she said, "'cause just when you think somethin's gonna be one way, it ends up another." Seems she was right. Which didn't surprise me none. She told me herself before she died.

"Lori Jean, your meemaw hasn't always been right, but she's never been wrong."

Mama and me, we wanted to put that on her gravestone. She'd of liked that, but it cost extra money, so Ray told them to just put her name on it, be done with it. He wasn't in too good a mood that day, so it's too bad it was her time to die that day 'cause she might would of had herself a nicer grave marker if'n she'd died the next week. Ray was whooping and hollering and real happy that week. That's when he come over and moved in with us. Mama give him all the money MeeMaw saved up in the jar and he took us all out to dinner for a celebration even. He probably might would of spent some of that money on a nicer grave marker for MeeMaw; I'm pretty sure he mighta, if she'd of died that week 'cause he sure was happy spreading all that money round town. He stayed that way for a couple a' weeks. When the jar got empty he got hisself in a bad mood again. Those days seemed so long ago. That was way before Melvin and Lexie had themselves any babies even.

"Uncle Melvin, I'd sure like to go with you to see Lexie and the baby tomorrow. It's Saturday. I don't got me any school."

"Well, baby girl, I wish you could, but they ain't about to let young'uns up on the floor."

"I'd be real quiet, I would. I promise," I said.

"Oh, I'm sure you would, Lori Jean. You're 'bout the best little girl I know." I loved it when Uncle Melvin said stuff like that about me. He made me feel real special, even if I wasn't.

"You see, sweet pea, it's not about being quiet. It's about bringing in them germs you young'uns carry around. That's why you can't visit."

"Oh," I said.

"You wouldn't want to get that new little baby sick now, would you?"

"No, sir. I surely would not," I said.

"Well, there you go then."

"But she's comin' home on Monday, you said. What about them germs I'll be carryin' around come Monday? Won't they make the baby sick, too?" I asked.

"Nah, by then that baby's got immunities from Lexie's milk."

"'Munnities? What's 'munnities?"

"Well, it's kinda hard to explain, Lori Jean, but I'll give it a shot." Uncle Melvin scratched at his whisker stubble and scrunched his forehead together.

"Immunities is, let me see now, immunities is, well, there's this little army of soldiers in your blood that fights with a little army a' soldiers in her blood."

"So her army's fightin' my army?"

"Yep."

"And that's good?"

"Yep! What do you think about that?"

"Alls I gotta say is if'n her army's fightin' my army, I sure hope she forgives me if my army wins."

Uncle Melvin burst out laughing like I was some kind of clown or something. We had us a fine old time. Being Friday night, Mama let me stay up late, even though her and Ray was tired and went to bed real early.

"Tell me again about you and Ray when you was growin' up, Uncle Melvin," I said.

"Those was pretty rough times, Lori Jean. What you want to hear about that for?" he asked.

"Well, I was hopin' it'd help me be nice to Ray the times he's bein' mean, knowin' what your pa done ta' him and all."

"Well, he's only mean as thunder when he's drunk, Lori Jean. He's sober right now. Let's just enjoy that, okay?"

He patted my head and squeezed past me to reach the whiskey bottle. He took the cork off and poured hisself a tad more. It was the white lightning he bought from old man Hawkins. Mr. Hawkins had one still left, way down yonder by the creek that Maybelle and the revenuers didn't know about. Poor Mr. Hawkins spent time in the jailhouse once a long time ago. Maybelle told on him and he got sent to work on the chain gang over in Jackson. That's how he come to be called old man Hawkins. He come out looking like an old man. Right before she called the law, Maybelle's pa died and left her all his money. So she didn't need Mr. Hawkins to support her none and she told him so. Said she'd put him there again, if'n he didn't mend his ways and follow the work of the Lord. He was pretty much scared of Maybelle. Mostly he did what she said, 'ceptin' for keepin' that one last still he had. I guess he figured it was worth it. MeeMaw said there's always something a body's fearless over.

"There's always one thing a body's willing to give their life for, Lori Jean," she said. "The lucky ones find what it is, but don't have to."

That still must of been the one for Mr. Hawkins 'cause he guarded it with his life, and he sure enough risked his freedom for it. Maybelle didn't abide by no lawbreaking—God's or man's. MeeMaw was that way, too, but she didn't believe in snitching on nobody.

"It's best to let the Lord do the correcting, Lori Jean," she told me. "He's the one keeping score, and he surely don't need my help."

MeeMaw had this here note on a piece of paper shaped like a heart she kept in her bureau drawer that said:

> *Dear Mavis,* [Mavis Edna Howard, that's her christened name]
>
> *I won't be needing any help today.*
> *Love, God*

When I asked why she kept it on top of her girdle, she said, "That way I see it every morning when I get my bloomers out and it reminds me to mind my own business." Mama said it pretty much didn't help her none. Said her heart was in the right place, but her nose never was; that she was always sticking it in where it didn't belong. 'Leastin' that's what Mama yelled at her when they used to fuss at each other, which weren't really that much, 'til Ray come around and MeeMaw didn't want Mama to have nothing to do with him.

"Uncle Melvin, my meemaw always said a man beats on a lady is a coward and deserves whatever sorrowful wrath the good Lord sends him. Is that true?" I asked.

"Well, baby girl, I'll tell ya'. It's not all that simple. Be nice if it were, though."

"What'cha mean?"

"Well, take your stepdaddy there. Now, I know when he drinks he gets mean as a monkey done lost his banana and your mama probably got in his way and got herself hurt a few times, but let me tell you, Ray's got a' sickness in him that's mostly the cause a' it. Now, I ain't sayin' that makes it right, and I surely ain't sayin' he ought to get away with it. All's I'm sayin' is, he's got defects that make it darned near impossible for him to be any other way."

"What'cha mean, defects?"

"He's got broken pieces inside him that never got fixed."

"You mean when your pa whipped him bad he broke bones inside his head that didn't mend and he's plumb crazy?"

"It's worse than that. Any bones he broke mostly healed that I know a'. The thing is, Lori Jean, our pa broke his spirit, cut right into his soul, scarred his insides for life, he did."

"What did he do to him?" I said. Melvin got hisself another whiskey.

"Ray loved to fish back in those days," Uncle Melvin said. "Stay down by a small lake ran out back . . ." He swallowed down more of that whiskey. "Stayed away for hours he did . . . anything not to be around . . ."

"But, what'd your pa do to him, Uncle Melvin?" I said.

"No need to be going over that," he said.

"I'd sure like to know, Uncle Melvin. So's I can understand. Maybe help him, if I can." Uncle Melvin was looking at me, but his eyes was far away.

"That old man . . . that old man . . ." Uncle Melvin said. "He . . . he . . ."

"He what?"

"He . . . liked to fish, Ray did. He sure did."

"But, what did your pa . . ."

"He went down to that lake whenever he could . . . Ray did . . . He . . . that old man . . . He was a good boy . . . Ray was . . . He . . . that old man . . . he . . . he . . ."

"But, what'd he do?" I said, trying to get him to tell me, but Uncle Melvin was froze still as a jackrabbit done seen a snake.

". . . He . . . he . . . ," Uncle Melvin whispered, "he . . . buggered him." I could barely hear him; only had me one good ear.

"For years that bastard . . . buggered him."

"Buggered?" I said. "What's *that*?"

"Don't be repeating that word, Lori Jean!" he said. "It ain't a nice thing."

"But, what is it?"

"Nothin'. Just forget I said anything."

"Please tell me, Uncle Melvin, please . . ."

"Lori Jean, it's something terrible he done to Ray."

"Well, just tell me what it is he done so's I won't ask no more." Uncle Melvin just sat there starin' off into space.

"He put his man part in Ray's butt!"

"His man part?" I said. "You mean like a man got a' part and a lady got a different part, that kind a' man part?"

"Yep," Melvin said.

"And he put it in Ray's butt?"

"Yep," Uncle Melvin said, and took hisself a big swallow of that whiskey.

"That don't sound right a'tall, Uncle Melvin," I said. "I don't reckon he oughta been doin' that."

"That's what you call one a' them understatements."

"Under who?"

"Never mind."

"Why'd he do it, Uncle Melvin?"

"I don't rightly know, Lori Jean. In all my years, I ain't never figured that out." Uncle Melvin got up and patted my shoulder.

"Oh," I said. He poured me another glass of that fine lemonade. "Well, maybe somebody done it to your pa and he grew up thinkin' it was a okay thing to do," I said.

"Maybe so, Lori Jean. Maybe so. It's too complicated for me. All's I know is Ray never got no love from that man, not ever." I set my lemonade down and it weren't even half gone.

"I shouldn't be talkin' about this to you, Lori Jean," he said. "What in thunder got into me?" Uncle Melvin grabbed the bottle of white lightning. He looked at it like he ain't been acquainted with it before. Then he stuck it up on the top shelf of the cabinet and slammed the door right in its face.

"I think I wanna go home now," I said. And I truly did. I wanted to go home and just forget everything Uncle Melvin told me. I kept seeing their pa's man part hurting Ray's butt when he was just a little fella and it was making my head sick and my heart hurt.

"Don't be repeatin' any a' what I told you, Lori Jean. It's family stuff."

"I won't," I said. "Uncle Melvin?"

"Uh-huh."

"You had that same pa. How come you ain't like Ray? How come you don't beat on nobody?"

"Well, for one, my pa never did those things to me, and for another, I reckon I got me a bit a' love along the way that carried me through."

"Didn't Ray get hisself any?" I asked.

"Probably did."

"Well, then how come he's not like you, Uncle Melvin?"

"Baby girl, I think he mighta needed a bit more than I did."

"Why?" I asked him.

"Some folks just do, Lori Jean," Melvin said.

I went on home to bed, thinking on what Melvin said about Ray needing more love than the rest of us. And I got me the answer to our troubles. If'n my mama and me could give Ray all the love he needed, then his head and his heart wouldn't be broken and hateful no more. Mama and me was just gonna have to love him up good. Heal him right up fine. We'd be a family, sure as church. Why, Ray was sleeping sober this very moment and hadn't had no liquor in him since the fire. He was almost cured for sure. We was so close to our dreams, I could smell the rust on the fenders of the old Chevy we'd git ourselves to fix up. That got me so excited I couldn't hardly sleep a'tall that night, thinking on how we'd drive into town, take that old car on over to Clyde Burt's dumpyard and pick us out some fenders could be painted good as new. They had a place in Marietta did that kind of thing. Carolee's pa, Morgan Thompson, had his done there. A 1949 Hudson come out looking like pretty brand-new. He had them paint it red, with a white top, he did. It had a big old ledge at the rear window. Carolee would climb up there and sleep all the way home from Atlanta when they went there to visit her cousin Eugenia and her uncle John and aunt Margaret. She was planning on me going with 'em sometime and I probably might would have if she hadn't gotten herself killed dead. That made me real sad, so I tried not to think about that part. I concentrated that night on dreams that might still could be. The chickens was close to clucking up a storm, wanting to get fed, when I finally went to sleep. It took me a while 'cause I was so happy thinking on the future we was getting ourselves.

If I had known what was gonna happen that next day, I'da been double sorrowful instead, so it's best we never know what's in store 'cause it would just ruin the time that comes before it for sure.

MeeMaw always said, "Lori Jean, enjoy every moment you can, 'cause you'll get plenty you can't." She sure was right. Saturday was one of them you can't, 'cause something terrible happened.

chapter eighteen

It started out like any other day. Mama had me get the eggs the chickens had laid while she fed 'em that morning. I was so tired out from not sleeping much I could barely drag myself off the cot. But Ray was going to work and he needed hisself a good breakfast for sure.

Mama fried him some eggs and fixed him bacon and toast. I poured his coffee and juice out nice for him and give him a kiss on his cheek, the side that weren't so scarred.

"Why, thank you, Lori Jean. How's my girl this morning?" he said. Fancy that! We was turning into a regular family we was, I'm telling ya'.

Mr. Jenkins done hired Ray full-time. Guess he felt sorry for him, 'cause before the fire he told Melvin he wouldn't hire him on account of talk was he might not show up regular. Mr. Jenkins's business was real good. Folks come from all over to buy his trailers. They was pretty much like new, once he got 'em fixed up. Some was much nicer than others, but those cost too much for us to get one of them. Ours only had one bedroom and a kitchen spot with a sink and two cabinets on each side, right next to a living room space. That's where I slept, on a cot we folded up during the day. It weren't real fancy, but it had a toilet inside with running water and a tub even. So that was pretty special for sure. The toilet was giving us trouble, but Ray, he was gonna work on it first chance he got. He and Melvin was gonna haul our old shed over on Melvin's pickup truck 'cause the fire didn't burn it none. Ray said we'd use it 'til the toilet worked good again.

That part about moving that shed give me heart failure. The flour sack with the money was under the back of the shed where a hole had caved in, right where I buried it the day of the fire. If Ray and Melvin dug all around to get the shed loose, they'd find it for sure. I was fixing to get that money back to the Scottsdale Cotton Mill where it belonged. I just hadn't worked out my plan yet. It was a long way to the mill.

Ray'd asked me about that flour sack that one time when they let me visit him in the hospital, and he asked me again the day he come home from the hospital. And then he asked about it that time he found bits of the sack by the porch, but that was it, so I figured he probably pretty much forgot about it and I had me plenty time to work on getting it back.

'Course he did go out and search through all our burned things at the house a few times. Made my belly drop to my innards, but he never did go near the shed that I knowed of, where we'd done our business the whole time we lived there. Probably 'cause it stunk bad, and for once I was glad about that.

Ray was fixing to move our trailer back there once we got us one of them fancy ones with two bedrooms and a nice big living area. Soon as we could get one a' them, we was gonna move he said. Those kind of trailers come with mostly new furniture even, and Mama was pretty excited, too. And I got so excited I jumped all around. Except I'da much rather we kept it parked next to Lexie and Melvin, but Ray said that's crazy, we own good land. Still I was real excited, I was.

"Calm down, Lori Jean. You're hoppin' around like a flea on a hot skillet," Mama said.

"Just think, Mama," I said, "we're gonna have us a fine place."

"It ain't happened yet." Then she started talking again about counting chickens 'fore they's hatched. That's her favorite, them chicken warnings. I tried to calm down some, but it was hard. I pretended to 'cause I wanted my mama to know I was trying to mind her good. She was trying to be a good mama, too, I think. It was just hard for her 'cause she had too much work to do. She didn't pay much attention to me, but she probably just couldn't find where to fit me in.

Even so, things was sorta looking up. But I did notice that Ray was getting pretty crabby after a few weeks of moving them heavy trailers. But you never know. Things might could still work out. Ray was asking Melvin a lot of questions about his Chevy. How much gas it took, stuff like that. Right then, we still had this old pickup truck that looked like the dickens. It was embarrassing to be seen in that thing, but most of the kids over at school still made fun of me over the clothes I wore, so I pretty much got over being embarrassed. Carolee used to tell 'em to shut up, told them they's just jealous 'cause my face was so pretty. Wasn't that nice a' her? 'Cause I'm sure my face was just regular; looked that way to me. You wouldn't have known it, though, to hear Carolee talk. She made me out to be Cinderella. I sure felt good when I was with her. I didn't care what names them kids called me. Now that Carolee was gone, they was back to their same old tricks, name-calling and stuff, but I was older and knew it didn't much matter. What did I care if they thought I was ugly? By then I knew I wasn't. Carolee give me that gift, and that's what really counted.

So whenever I climbed in that truck with Ray and Mama, I tried not to let it bother me. That morning I was counting all my blessings for what I had. Me and Mama was sweeping the dirt yard up nice. Right then Melvin come driving up that long dirt road that led to the trailers. He come flying out of the car, yelling for Mama.

"Nadine, Lexie needs you at the hospital! She's about half crazy, she is!" he said.

"Melvin Pruitt, what in the dickens . . ." Uncle Melvin didn't really let her get a word in crosswise.

"Somethin's happened to the baby. They ain't exactly told us what, but Lexie's gone plumb nuts and they had to give her a shot. It ain't helped none and they're fixin' to take her up to the nut ward if she don't settle down. Had to tie her to the bed."

"Sweet Jesus, what happened?" my mama yelled.

"Just git in the car, Nadine. Git in the car!" Melvin was yelling even louder than my mama.

"Mama, let me come, too," I begged. "Please let me come." But they was gone so fast the tires spun chunks of dirt onto the weeds growing alongside the road.

I run all the way over to Maybelle Hawkins's, see if she'd call the hospital for me and find out what happened. She don't like no one making any long-distance calls on her phone, but she probably might would this time 'cause she's so nosey and she'd want to know all about Lexie and who tied her to the bed and what for and stuff. But when I got over there these men from the telephone company was stringing this line back up to her house, looked kind of like a long rubber jump rope. They was busy hooking it up right next to her porch.

Maybelle come out the back door when I got there.

"What's the trouble, Lori Jean? You're clean out a' breath and filthy as leftover dishwater."

"I got to git on over to the the hospital where Lexie is, Mz. Hawkins. Somethin' terrible's happened." I told her what I knew.

"Well, come on then," she said. She grabbed my arm and headed for her barn where she kept her car. It was a big Oldsmobile. She left it in there, I think, 'cause she didn't do no farming anymore. Ever since her daddy died and left her a passel of money, mostly she just looked like a farmer's wife, but she weren't. She just liked living there. It was where she was born. She liked the money her pa left her, too, and she spent lots of it, but folks said no matter how much she spent she'd never run out, that's how much her daddy left her. I don't know if that part's true, though, 'cause when people from the church asked for money to help out the poor folks, she never give much, so that part about not running out's probably not true. And she fretted about money all the time, telling us how much everything costs and for me and Mama to be careful when we dusted her things. She sure had a whole lot of pretty things. Every time we finished dusting them it was time to start dusting them again. One time I told Mama, "I don't ever want this much stuff. It's too much trouble." Now with Lexie and little Iris Anne in some kind of trouble, I knew there was other reasons not to worry over having stuff. There was things much more important for sure.

Maybelle weren't too happy to have me in her car on the ride to the hospital. My coveralls was pretty dirty, so I didn't much blame her. She spread out a dishtowel for me to sit on.

"Now don't move around none, ya' hear?"

"Yes, ma'am," I said. I set real still like, as best I could, and tried hard not to move even when I got me an itch right in the middle of my back. But I couldn't help it; it got the best of me and I had to rub myself real hard against the back seat cushion.

"Sit still, Lori Jean! Don't go rubbin' all that dirt into my upholstery."

"I can't help it, ma'am. I got me an itch," I said.

"An itch? Good Lord! You best not have any bugs. I don't want any bugs in my car."

"No, ma'am," I said. "I don't got any bugs, just 'squito bites. I got me a bunch a' them."

"Well, sit still. You can scratch all you want when we get there."

I tried not to move none. If I hadn't been so upset over what Melvin said about Lexie and the baby and I wasn't all tickly from them 'squito bites, it would of been a special day 'cause I always wanted to ride in Maybelle's car. It was real shiny. Some kids from school might could a' seen me riding in that fine automobile. That would've been something, but I was too worried about Lexie to think about it.

Turns out Melvin and Lexie's little baby, Iris Anne, died that morning. Nobody could tell 'em why. One of the nurses found her. She was in one of them cute little beds you can see clean through the sides of. She'd already turned blue. They tried to git her to breathe, but she must not wanted to 'cause she didn't blow any air back at 'em when they put their mouths over hers, 'cluding her nose and breathed lots of air into her. They told Melvin they did that for a long time, breathed in her mouth and nose, but it didn't do no good.

Seems Lexie come down to where the babies was that morning. It had a window with a big sign above it said NURSERY. It was so the daddies could see their new young'uns and how big they was and show 'em off to folks that come by. It was real early. It wasn't even light out yet. By then them nurses was shaking Iris all about and yelling for the doctors, and Lexie, she seen them. She just burst right in and yanked

Iris Anne out of their arms and wouldn't let go. Them nurses told her to put the baby down.

"It's dead!" they yelled. "It's dead!" Imagine that? No wonder Lexie lost her mind. The doctors come and give her this powerful shot, Melvin said, before they could pry the baby from her, and then they took her back to her room.

"When she woke up they had to tie her to the bed," he said, "'cause she wouldn't stay put. She was wailing so loud the doctors said to take her to the nervous ward, she was scaring the other mothers." Melvin was so upset.

"They put this straitjacket on her and tied it so tight, she near couldn't breathe," Uncle Melvin said. When he got there it was mostly over. They didn't have no telephone number to reach him at and was waiting on him to show up for a visit. Turns out, Riley Davis, that worked at the hospital heard the commotion and knew Melvin. He told 'em Melvin worked at Jenkins' Trailerama when he weren't workin' at the mill, so them hospital folks sent the sheriff deputy on over to Mr. Jenkins's place to tell Melvin to get to the hospital quick. 'Course Melvin done like he said to. Knowing Uncle Melvin, he was probably worried sick to death, 'cause he loved Lexie more than any man I knowed of loved a woman.

When Melvin got to the hospital he wanted to take Lexie out of that place, but they told him he couldn't, not until they was sure she wasn't a danger to herself. They had her on a special watch where they thought she'd kill herself. Melvin was so mad. They put her in this room where the walls was padded and they took away all her clothes.

When we got to the hospital they told us to wait in this little room for the doctor to come and talk to us. That's when Uncle Melvin told Mama what they done to Lexie. Then he cried like a baby. I felt bad having Maybelle there with us seeing that. She weren't family or nothing. I think she was uncomfortable, too. She kept saying things nobody much wanted to hear.

"Now now, let's look on the bright side. No sense being downhearted," she said. Then later she said, "Probably something was wrong with that baby. I understand it's nature's way of being merciful. Probably for the best it was." That was just too much for Mama. She like ta' let her have it.

"Mz. Hawkins, it was real nice a' you to bring Lori Jean and I don't want to be disrespectful to you or nothin', but we don't need you addin' to our grief."

"Well, excuse me! I'm just giving my opinion, Nadine," Maybelle said real snippy like.

"Listen, you old woman, you give us one more a' your opinions, I'm gonna give you one a' mine." Mama made herself a fist and aimed it right at Mz. Hawkins. "I'm gonna stuff it right down your throat."

"Don't be getting all smart with me, Nadine. I'll call the law."

Things was heating up real good. Uncle Melvin put a halt to it.

"Stop it, the both a' you. Ain't we got enough trouble here?" he said. He used his big hands and wiped his face off. His eyes was all bulgy and red.

"Where's Ray, Mama? Ain't Ray comin'?" I said.

"He's fixin' to dig around the outhouse now the ground's all soggy from the rain. Ain't no one drove out to tell him what's happened," she said.

I must of turned white as a Klansman when she said he was gonna dig around our old outhouse.

"You okay, Lori Jean?" Mama asked. "You don't look so good, honey."

I didn't feel even as good as I might of looked. I never did make it out to the shed to take the money and bury it somewhere else on account of all that rain we'd been having. Ray'd find it for sure.

"Mz. Hawkins," I said, "could you take me on home? I feel right poorly, I do."

"Well, I don't know. Seems I'm not appreciated by this family," Maybelle said. She looked right at Mama when she said it, 'stead of at me.

"Oh, Mz. Hawkins," I said, "you surely are 'preciated. You're definitely the most 'preciated person I knows right now."

"That's only 'cause you want something. I won't be taken advantage of," she said.

"No ma'am. Surely not. I'm gonna come help you today, I am. Soon as I feel better. I need to get home and rest so I'll get better and then I can come help you," I said. "For free even. On account a' you givin' me a ride and all." I was gonna beg her if I had to. I had to get out to the shed before Ray did.

"But we gotta hurry. I'm gettin' sicker by the minute, I am."

"Not until your mama apologizes to me, young lady," Maybelle said. Mama sat there all quiet like.

"Come here, Lori Jean," she said. "Let me feel your forehead. You got yourself a fever?"

"Yes, Mama, I surely must. I'm feelin' real bad, I'm tellin' ya'." Which weren't a lie. I was. Mama felt my forehead with her hand, then she leaned her cheek against it to check it better.

"You're burnin' up!" she said. Fancy that. I must of been burning up with fear 'cause I weren't regular sick or nothing. I was plumb sick to death over what might could happen to us all if Ray found that money.

"I must be, Mama. I'm feelin' mighty hot," I said. I give her the most pitiful look I could muster.

"You best tell Mz. Hawkins how sorry you are, Mama, for

sayin' them sorrowful things to her. Best tell her you didn't mean it," I said. Mama sat pursing her lips.

"It was grief talkin' for sure, don't you think, Mama?" I said. Mama looked over at Mz. Hawkins, who was sitting with her nose in the air.

"Maybelle, I'm rightly sorry for what I said. I know you was just tryin' to be a help and here I was bein' a nilly," Mama said. Maybelle just sat there.

"Please forgive me my foolishness, Maybelle. You always been right good to us and I'm sorry. I truly am." Tears was welling up in Mama's eyes. Maybelle still sat there with her chin all stiff like and tipped upward. I didn't mind begging Maybelle for help, but I didn't want my mama to have to.

"That was a right nice 'pology, wasn't it, Mz. Hawkins?" I asked.

"Humph!" Maybelle said.

"You can be sure my mama means every word a' it. She's a good Christian lady and you is, too. And God's probably smilin' down on both a' ya's right now for making friends." I think Maybelle's face softened a little bit.

"He probably's fixin' to bless ya' good. Send somethin' right nice your way 'cause he sure likes forgiveness. He sure enough does." Maybelle smiled at me.

"One a' his favorite things, it is," I said, "forgiveness."

"All right, all right. Let's get going," Maybelle said.

"Yes, ma'am." I kissed Mama and Uncle Melvin goodbye.

We headed on out to Maybelle's car. It took forever. It was barely spring, but it was muggy outside and Maybelle sure took her time. She had a little fan she kept brushing back and forth in front of her face. We needed to hurry and here she was moseying along like she was strolling a baby carriage, not a care in the world. Meanwhile, me and Mama's world was coming to an end.

We made it to the car and I breathed me one a' them sighs of relief.

"I need to stop at the market on the way home. Pick up a few things," Maybelle said.

"Oh, Mz. Hawkins. That's not a good idea. I wouldn't want to get sick in your nice car," I said. "We best get me straight home 'fore I puke."

"I'll get you a grocery bag and you can put your head in it," she said. "I'm not making two trips." And that's what she done. She come back a bit later with a paper sack for me to stick my head in. Then she went back inside and didn't come out for what seemed like hours, but probably weren't. She had a grocery boy in tow. He loaded her things into the trunk and she give him a quarter.

"You're a nice young man. And fancy that, you being Verna Louis's boy! Why I haven't seen your mama since grade school," Maybelle said. "Now you tell her I said hello and give her my number. Tell her to call me. Married herself a doctor, you say?"

"Yes, ma'am. Daddy's got a big practice over in Carrollton."

"Well, what are you doin' way over here in Decatur then, Clayton?" Maybelle asked. Good grief, time was running short and Maybelle done run into kin of someone she knew when she was a girl, and here she was trying to fill in all them years in between. No telling how long she'd be once she got going.

"Mama's sister took sick and I come to live with her. Help her out around the house," that Clayton fella said. He seemed right nice. Had a nice face, too. Exceptin' for his teeth. They was bucked and stuck out of his mouth even when he closed it.

"Yes, ma'am. She's all alone. Her husband died last year. She never had any children."

"My, my," Maybelle said. "That wouldn't be Stella, would it?"

"No, ma'am. Aunt Stella died years back."

"I'm so sorry to hear that."

"Thank you, ma'am."

"What happened to poor Stella?"

"Her appendix ruptured."

"That's so sad," Maybelle said. "You tell your mama I'm real sorry to hear that."

"I will, ma'am."

"So you're staying with your mama's older sister then? What's her name . . ."

"Ruth Anne."

"That's right, I remember. She's older than your mama. Graduated, she did, before your mama and I even made it outa grammar school."

"Yes ma'am. A lot older."

"Well, here's my number . . ." Maybelle handed him a slip of paper. "Give that to your mama. Don't forget now."

"I won't, ma'am."

"And tell her . . ."

"Mz. Hawkins," I called out. "I'm feelin' so pitiful. Can we hurry?"

"Oh, my! I almost forgot. Got a sick neighbor child to take home," Maybelle said. That Clayton fella glanced at me in the car. Maybelle cupped her hand to her mouth and whispered, "Poor white trash from Elmer County," but I heared her.

"Her mama works for me. I'm helpin' them out a bit," she said and waved goodbye before she climbed in the car. I wasn't going to get over to the shed before Ray did. Too much time had passed. Ray got off work Mondays at noon; that was their slow day, and here it was almost one o'clock and we still had to drive all the way back home and then I had to make it over to our old place on foot. I'd need me one a' them miracles and we'd already got one what with Irl getting well. I didn't rightly think God was gonna give me another one. He had a lot of other folks to tend to and they deserved miracles, too. I couldn't hardly ask him for another one, but I sure wanted to. And I sure should have 'cause that day marked the beginning of the end.

chapter nineteen

"Isn't that beat-up rattletrap Ray's truck, Lori Jean?" Mz. Hawkins asked.

"Why, it surely is," I said. I was getting me a miracle after all. Ray's truck was stuck in the mud at the side of the road. Looked like his reckless driving finally paid off good. He run off the road and got hisself stuck real bad. Maybelle pulled over.

"What happened, Ray?" she asked.

"What in thunder do you think happened? Fool woman."

"Don't be gettin' all nasty with me, Ray Pruitt. I got your girl here. Taking her home sick." Ray didn't say nothing. Just kept digging at the back tire with a shovel.

"Mama's at the hospital with Uncle Melvin, Ray. Little Iris Anne died this mornin'."

"She did now, did she?" Ray said, like it made no difference to him none. "Well, these things happen."

"I think Mama needs you, Ray. Mz. Hawkins can call the sheriff deputy man when she gets home. He'd come git you and take you on over to the hospital. Then you can git your truck later when Uncle Melvin can help ya'. Don't you think?" I asked.

"They're ain't nothin' I can do. No sense in me goin'," he said.

"Sure there is. Mama needs you real bad. She's right sad. 'Bout fallin' apart, she is," I said. Ray got in the truck and run the engine good. All it did was dig the back tires deeper into the ruts he dug.

"Goddamnit!" he said. "Go ahead and call them deputies. But tell 'em to just bring Melvin out here so's I can get this goddamn truck outa here."

"No sense usin' that kind a' language, Ray Pruitt. Show some respect," Mz. Hawkins said. "I got a right mind to leave you to your troubles. Filthy mouth and all."

"Well, excuse me, Maybelle," Ray said and took his cap off. He bowed over at the waist.

"Please send the good deputy on over to get Melvin so he can help me get this fine truck outa this nice mudhole." He slapped the sides of his overhauls and put his cap back on and smiled at her, but it was a smart-mouth kind of smile.

We drove on off. I looked out the rear window and Ray was sticking his finger up in the air at her.

"He's givin' you the middle finger, Mz. Hawkins," I said. "I think you should leave him to his troubles, don't you?"

"Humph!" she said.

If she didn't send no one to help him, I'd have me plenty of time to do what I had to do at the shed. Maybelle dropped me off.

"Thank you kindly, Mz. Hawkins," I said. "I'll be over to help you like I promised once I feel better."

"Well, get some rest, child," Maybelle said and drove off. I got my dirty overhauls out of the basket of clothes Mama and me was fixing to wash that afternoon and put 'em on quick like. There wasn't a minute to spare nohow.

Once I got to the shed I found out the flour sack had mostly fell apart in that soggy ground; rotted near clean away. I gathered it up as best I could and drug it and the money into the woods. I had to make me several trips 'cause the bills kept falling out along the way. I found me a tree had the bottom all hollowed out. I rolled up the sack as best I could and stuck it inside. I piled on sticks and leaves and whatever ground cover I could muster to put on top. Then I packed it down real good. It sure was a relief. Now I just had to get it back to the cotton mill and everything would be okay. Ray and Mama and me could work on being a family. It's hard to be a family if'n a pa's on a chain gang, even a step-pa. When I got home Mama was there waiting on me.

"Where you been, Lori Jean? I been worried sick." She come out on the platform and stood with her arms crossed in front of the trailer door.

"I thought maybe a walk in the woods would clear my head, break my fever good," I said.

"Why, that's crazy talk. You best come in and lie down a spell."

"Yes, Mama," I said.

"And just look at you, plumb full a' dirt. Looks like you rolled in them woods."

I didn't make it over to Mz. Hawkins's that day. Mama made me stay in and rest. Fed me bread in a bowl with milk and sugar sprinkled on top. But it was hard acting sick when I wasn't. All the while, Mama was busy making arrangements for us to bury Iris Anne. The day of the funeral was my birthday. I was ten. Mama took care of everything. She got the church folks to let us bury Iris Anne in the cemetery plot right on top of MeeMaw. They said we could put her there on account there was plenty a' room. They was probably right.

Ray said MeeMaw was six feet under. If he was telling the truth for once, might be room enough for me someday 'cause Melvin said Iris Anne was only twenty-one inches long. Six feet, that's a lot of room. Might could put us all there.

At the cemetery we all crowded around in a circle. Everyone but Lexie. She didn't get out of the hospital 'til the next day. I think Melvin planned it so she wouldn't be there for the burying. He knew Lexie wouldn't want to see little Iris Anne packed down into the ground, when just a few weeks before she was carrying that little baby around in her belly, feeling her kick. The preacher come and give a blessing.

"Lord, we commit this child to eternal peace. May she rest in your loving care, residing safely in your arms for all eternity. May you comfort those who would prefer that she remain and remind them of your promise that we shall all meet again in everlasting paradise."

We was all pretty much crying by then. Even Mama. I wondered why she didn't cry over little Paulie, who probably would have been a right fine brother to me. Maybe she was so grieved by my real pa running off, she couldn't think straight about anything else. We laid out some flowers on top of the dirt mound for Iris Anne. Then we sung "Amazing Grace" 'cause we didn't have no hymnals with us, and we knew the words to that song. Then we left. The sun wasn't shining at all and black clouds was rolling in. Seems sadness was everywhere that day. Guess even heaven didn't like taking no baby girl away so soon, even though it was the one getting her.

Mama said we'd do something for my birthday later, but we wasn't fixing to have no regular birthday party or nothing like Carolee had herself 'fore she died. We was still getting over the fire and Iris Anne's passing.

I spent that morning helping Mz. Hawkins like I always did

on weekends. I knew it was the perfect chance for me to ask for her help in taking the money back. I was hoping she'd feel a bit sorrowful for us, what with all the troubles our family was having; that she'd take pity on us and help me. Plus, it being my birthday, she might like to do something nice for me. Never know.

"Mz. Hawkins," I said, "supposin' somebody was in trouble and needed help and was real sorrowful for their trouble. Would you help 'em?"

"Well, I always been a Christian lady. It'd be my duty to help now, wouldn't it?"

"That's what I figure," I said. "See, I need me some help, Mz. Hawkins, but I don't rightly want you to ask me no questions 'cause it's real serious trouble."

"Well now, Lori Jean, I can't rightly help unless you tell me how it is I can help you."

"Well, Mz. Hawkins, I just need you to drive me on over to Decatur for a piece is all."

"I can't be gallivanting all over Georgia without knowing why now, can I? Hardly seems right."

"But it's a secret, Mz. Hawkins. I ain't told no one."

"You can tell me, Lori Jean. I'm not going to tell anyone. I'm going to help you, remember?" She was making it sound so easy. I should of asked her weeks ago when Ray was in the hospital. We finished folding up the laundry. I stacked it up nice and put it in the wicker basket.

"Reckon I should take this on up to the linen closet, Mz. Hawkins?"

"Oh, just leave that be, Lori Jean. I'll get it myself later." She was being so nice. It was my lucky day and here it was my birthday, too. Things was gonna be perfect. Mama was home baking a cake and getting everything ready for a nice supper with Aunt Lexie and Uncle Melvin and the twins. Little Irl was home from the hospital and learning to walk again with these braces they put on his legs. The doctors said he was one tough little fella. He was gonna be fine. Might even be able to do without braces someday. Mama said Lexie would get over losing Iris Anne eventually, probably have herself another baby even.

"Nothin' like a new little baby to help heal wounds, Lori Jean," she said.

"'Course that won't ever replace little Iris, but all babies bring their own joy into this world. God knows we need some, after all we been through this year," Mama said that morning 'fore I left for Mz. Hawkins's.

Now the day could really be perfect. I'd take that sack of money back to the mill and go on home to a fine birthday supper. If we was lucky Ray wouldn't get too drunk. He was back to drinking most every night again. He started up again when the doctor wouldn't give him no more pain pills; said he didn't need 'em no more. Mama was beside herself. But I wasn't going to let his drinking spoil my day. No sirree. Now, if only Mz. Hawkins would help me, then things could be perfect. I'd have me a really fine day.

"Go on, Lori Jean. Tell me why we're going to Decatur. I ain't got all day," Maybelle said. As much as I wanted to tell her and get on with it, something inside held me back.

"Lori Jean, didn't you tell me today's your birthday?"

"Yes, ma'am," I said.

"Well then, shake a leg. Don't you want to get home to your family?"

"I surely do. Mama's havin' a supper for me with Uncle Melvin and Aunt Lexie and the twins. We're havin' cake and maybe ice cream, too."

"Well, there you go. You need to tell me what's what and be done with it, girl."

"Mz. Hawkins, I need you to take me on over to the Scottsdale Cotton Mill so's I can take the money back I found in a flour sack the day of the fire." I spit it all out in one breath.

"You found what?" Mz. Hawkins's mouth dropped open.

"I found the payroll money that was took from the mill. Ray done stole it when he was drunk, Mz. Hawkins. I got to get it back so we can be a family."

"You mean that money they're giving a five-hundred-dollar reward for?"

"Yes, ma'am. That very money."

"Lori Jean, you wait right here. I'll be right back. I'll just make a telephone call and clear all this up. That's just what I'll do. You wait right here. Just one little telephone call," she said.

Mz. Hawkins got up and went out to her kitchen. I knew her phone was out there hung on the wall. At first, I was sorely relieved. But then, I got me a bit nervous. I started remembering all the things I should of remembered 'fore I told her my secret. Like how much she liked money and never could seem to get enough. And five hundred dollars' reward was a whole bunch of money to get. And I was remembering what Aunt Lexie told me at the fair about her causing more trouble than a hurricane that hits in the night. The more I thought about it, the more nervous I got. I knew I'd made me a big mistake. I sneaked around the corner and seen Maybelle take the phone off the hook. She put her finger on the big black dial and dialed the first number. Then she dialed the second number. Only two more to go and whoever she was calling would be on the line. As much as I wanted to, I just couldn't chance that who she was calling was somebody who would help me. I run outside to where them men strung that rubber line up to her house and I tried to yank it clean out of the box it was hooked up to, but it wouldn't budge. I pulled as hard as I could, but it didn't do no good. Whoever hooked it up the day they fixed it oughta get a raise for sure. They done a really good job.

chapter twenty

I took off running to our old place to dig up the money. A storm had been brewing all morning and just about then it got real nasty. Streaks of lightning flashed across the sky and it weren't long the thunder started in. Then the rain come down and drenched me good. I wasn't having me a very good day after all.

When I got to the outhouse I slipped down on my knees and used my hands to dig at the muddy ground, hoping to get at the flour sack stuck in the hole. But all I found was bits and pieces of it and a couple a' soggy ten-dollar bills. I was just plumb full of panic and my mind wasn't working good. Then I remembered I'd moved the money that day Mz. Hawkins brought me home from the hospital when Iris Anne died. I put it there in the woods in the hollow of an old tree trunk. I thought I'd been right careful that day to pick up every stray bill that fell out of that pitiful sack. I seen now I missed some and I left big soggy pieces of what was left of that flour sack, too. They was stuck in the muddy dirt all around the edge of the shed. I gathered up bits and pieces of the flour sack and what money was there and stuffed it into my overhauls.

"Where's the rest a' it, you little shit?" A big thunder of a voice boomed out and I looked up at the black sky above me, fixing to see who coulda said it. Was it God? If it were, he was plenty mad 'cause he done said the poop word!

"I said where's the rest a' it?" It was Ray. He come staggering out of the trees on the far side of the outhouse.

"You told me that sack burned, girl." He come at me so fast I near froze in my tracks.

"You lied," he said. He grabbed hold of my shoulder. "Where's the money?" He grabbed a fistful of my hair, wound it tight around his hand and jerked my head back so hard I bit my tongue.

"Where is it?" he screamed into my good ear. 'Fore I had me a chance to answer, he flung me to the ground. A big chunk of my hair got left with him. It stuck right there to his fingers. His hands was all full of mud. He'd probably been digging round the outhouse to loosen it up so's he and Uncle Melvin could move it over to our place, and he musta seen some of them bills I left behind.

"I come here, Lori Jean, mindin' my own business, fixin' to get this here outhouse moved, and what do you think I find me?" he asked. "Huh? What'd I find, girl?" I didn't answer. I started scrambling to my feet.

"You lied to me, girl! You hid that money, and all this time you been lyin' to me. All this time I been workin', movin' them trailers, bustin' my back, and you been sittin' on my money." Ray come at me and kicked me straight in the belly. A pain cut through me so sharp I thought his foot was a knife. It cut into me so bad I couldn't talk. I couldn't tell him I kept it so I could take it back. So's we'd be a family.

He kicked me again. I started to moan something awful; it hurt me so bad. He kicked me over and over on my backside real low below my waist. I throwed up all over the ground.

"Ray," I whispered, "I was takin' it back so . . . I was . . ."

He jerked me to my feet. More pain shot down my spine and into my legs.

". . . takin' it back so we could be a family and you wouldn't go to the chain gang . . . so you wouldn't get in no trouble . . . ,'"

"'I was takin' it back so you wouldn't get in no trouble . . ." he mimicked me. "Trouble is what you're gonna get if I don't get my money. Where is it?" He punched me hard in the belly three times in a row. I didn't know a person could throw up as hard as I did then. It come outa me so fast it went flying through the air like water shooting out a garden hose.

"I hid it," I said, but it come out real soft; don't know if he heard. Snot and blood come out, too.

"I hid it. But I'll git it for you. I will. Let me go, Ray! Let me go! I'll git it for you," I said over and over but them words still come out so quiet, they was hardly even a whisper.

"Let's go," he said.

I limped about trying to remember where the money was with Ray at my heels. My mind was playing this trick on me and wouldn't tell me which part of them woods I hid it. I stumbled from this place to that place to another place and dug with my fingers at all of them, but couldn't find the sack.

"I can't remember, Ray," I said. "It's here somewhere, it is. I just can't remember."

"You're lyin! Git me that money!"

"Honest, Ray, I ain't lyin'," I said. "I ain't. I promise you, I ain't."

"Give me that money!" Ray beat at my face. He punched me like I seen them cowboys do in the movies. I keeped landing on my backside each time he swung at me. But every time I hit the ground, Ray grabbed me up and hit me again. I felt my jaw crack. And when I tried to tell him one more time I wasn't lying, my mouth didn't work. I reached up to touch it. It was wide open and my chin just dangled like one a' them ornaments hung from a tree. Bits of my teeth fell into my hand and I coughed up some blood. My ears roared like them waterfalls I visited once with MeeMaw at Tallulah Falls. I couldn't hear what Ray was saying no more, neither. I seen him forming words on his lips, but my ears didn't work, not even my good one. Strange thing, the beating Ray was giving me was wearing him down. I could tell he was breathing hard by the way his chest was moving up and down, and he was staggering about in a circle trying to catch his breath. That was my chance.

I took off running and kept going 'til my legs give out and I dropped down in the tall grass by the creek. The ground was so soggy, my shoulders and feet sunk right in. I curled up on my side and rocked my tummy and sucked in that Georgia red clay 'til it clung like perfume that wouldn't let go.

Then something mighty peculiar happened. All them places on my body that hurt me so bad started to not hurt me so bad no more. And the sky, it was swirling with these pretty lights, and the ground wasn't cold and wet like it were when I fell. 'Fore long I wasn't even on the ground no more. I was floating on pillows soft as clouds. Imagine that! And that blanket of barbed wire that wrapped me tight snapped off and a comforter thick and warm as a jacket of goose feathers took its place. The roaring in my ears stopped, too. And my teeth weren't jagged on my tongue no more, neither. Fancy that! I laid there and rested myself good for quite a spell.

It took me a while, but eventually I knowed I wasn't part of their world no more; the one Ray and Mama and Uncle Melvin and Aunt Lexie lived in. I wasn't part of it, but I was near it. I watched from a place, soft and peaceful, a place full of light, far off, but close enough to see and hear everything. It was something, I'm telling ya'. I wasn't really there, yet I was. I could hear, but they couldn't hear me. I could talk, but they couldn't talk back. I called over and over. No one answered.

Ray come looking for me then. He yelled, his voice filled with liquor.

"Lori Jean! You git back here! Ya' hear me?" he said. I heared him, but I didn't answer. He found me then; stumbled over me in the grass. He yanked me up by my hair, but I didn't move. That's when he seen—I couldn't walk. I couldn't breathe. That's when he changed his tune. He dropped down on his knees and held me so nice. He had his arms wrapped all around me and he was hugging me to his chest, just like a regular daddy, just like I always wanted him to.

"Oh my girl, my sweet baby girl," he said over and over. I watched him carry me down to Roseflower Creek and dump me in the water. There I was, floating on a cloud, floating in the river, right in the middle of the creek! Ray took off running and I followed him home. It was mighty peculiar. He couldn't tell I was there. And my body didn't have to move to go with him, but I could see everything going on, plain as church.

Mama was busy setting the table for my birthday supper. She'd made a roast and boiled potatoes and collard greens and corn bread. There was carrots next to the roast and gravy in a pan on the stove. My cake didn't have any frosting, but it had sugar sprinkled on the top with ten candles. Looked real fine.

"Nadine, pack your bag. We gotta get outa here," Ray said when he burst in the door of the trailer. Mama whirled around.

"What in blue heaven are you talkin' about, Ray?"

"Don't be askin' no questions, Nadine. I'm the man of this family, and I say we gotta clear out of here!" He grabbed Mama by the hair, spun her around and shoved her towards the back of the trailer where the bedroom was.

"Git! Git yore stuff. Git it now or leave it. Either way, we're goin'." Mama had gotten some of her old spunk back while Ray was recuperating from the fire, and I think she might of give him some trouble about leaving, but when she seen the look in his eye something must of told her to go along with him. She went and grabbed a few things and stuck 'em in a pillowcase.

"We got to go on over to Mz. Hawkins's and get Lori Jean," she said. Mama folded the pillowcase in half and laid my sweater and extra coveralls on top.

"And we should stop by Melvin and Lexie's. Tell 'em supper's off, too. You ain't forgot it's Lori Jean's birthday, have you?" she asked. "This supper I fixed here is for her." Mama pointed to all the fixin's.

Ray shoved Mama out the door of the trailer. "We can't be worried 'bout no supper right now. Get in the truck." Mama climbed up on the front seat of the truck. He slammed the door shut behind her.

"Can't you tell me what's goin' on at least, Ray? We got a life here," Mama yelled out the window as he run to the other side of the truck.

"We don't got nothin', woman, if we don't get outa' here."

"Someone after you, Ray? Did somethin' happen with Mr. Jenkins? Huh?" Ray didn't answer. He put the truck in gear and tore off down the dirt road, but when he got to the end of it he didn't head towards town like he always done before. He turned onto the part of the road that led up to Sugarville. There weren't nothing up there but backroads and woods and a bunch of abandoned shacks from when people got tired of looking for gold MeeMaw said probably wasn't there to begin with.

"If ya' done somethin' wrong, Ray, it's best we face it. There ain't no sense in runnin', Ray," Mama said. "We kin . . ."

"Shut up!" Ray yelled. "Shut up!" He swung his right arm out and smacked her good on the side of her face.

"I can't think straight with you runnin' yore mouth." It was then Mama noticed what direction he was going in.

"Ray! Turn around! Turn around! We gotta git Lori Jean!" she said.

"We'll have to have Melvin bring her to us later. They're ain't no time right now." That's when Mama started to wail.

"Oh, God, oh, God! What's goin' on?" She was crying and carrying on something terrible. I knowed then she loved me like she done loved MeeMaw. I sure felt good about that. But that lying no-count Ray, he told her Melvin could bring me up to wherever they was headed, and that was one his lies for sure 'cause I weren't around to bring nowhere to nobody no more. I knew when my mama found out what he done to me she'd probably not want to be going with him ever again. That part would suit me fine. We never got to be no family nohow. Ray done brought Mama a lot of heartache and he was fixin' to dump some more on her. She deserved someone better than him. She deserved someone like Uncle Melvin who'd take care of her and love her up right. And here we'd been trying to give Ray all the love he done missed when he was a little boy, and it didn't do a lick of good.

They drove until they was on empty and Ray stopped at a filling station in a little town called McCoy. A man come out with dirty overhauls and a dirty cap to match. His name was written on the top of his overhauls in red thread. *Chester* it said.

He was sucking on a toothpick. He pushed it to the side of his mouth with his tongue when he talked. He never once choked on it, so he'd probably been sucking on toothpicks a long time.

"Howdy, folks," he said. "Fill 'er up?"

"Nah, just give me a dollar's worth," Ray said. He looked through his wallet, then closed it up. Mama stayed in the truck dabbing at her eyes. A nasty bruise was forming on her cheek where Ray punched at her.

"Me and the Mrs. is takin' a bit of a holiday. Git away from the kids fer a spell; have us a little fun," Ray said and winked when he said the word *fun.*

"You know anybody got a place we could stay at?" The man called Chester scratched his head.

"Nothin' fancy, now. Somethin' don't cost too much money," Ray said. "I got more sense than money and my woman here says I ain't got much a' that." Ray and the fella shared a laugh. But that fella Chester didn't laugh like his heart was in it, and he kept staring at my mama when Ray wasn't looking. He might of been the kind of person can tell when something just ain't right. MeeMaw said there's folks like that. They got extra-special senses or something. Then there's these kinds of peoples can tell when a person's character is good or not just by standing next to 'em, MeeMaw said. Seems maybe this Chester fella was both these kind of people all at once. He sure didn't seem to cotton to Ray none. Funny thing, Ray didn't seem to notice it, but I sure did. I think Mama did, too, 'cause she kept looking at this fella, pleading at him with her eyes when Ray wasn't watching. Her eyes was kind of saying, *Help me, please help me*—that kind of look.

The Chester fella cleaned their windshield while the gas was pumping.

"George Johnson's got an old fishin' shack he don't use no

more since his arthritis got too bad. Might could stay there a spell," Chester said.

"Now how would I get a hold a' this Mr. Johnson? We gotta hurry," Ray said.

Chester looked up when Ray said that.

"We ain't got a lotta time 'fore I got to be back to work. We're anxious to git where we're goin', git our holiday started," Ray told Chester. Chester nodded polite like.

"Where you folks from?" he asked.

"Macon," Ray said, and that was a lie. We ain't never come from Macon.

"Macon. That's a pretty far piece for a short holiday," Chester said.

"We kept drivin' along. 'Fore we knew it we was here," Ray said. "Now this Mr. Johnson fella . . ."

"He's over at the coffee shop. Just take this road into town a piece." Chester pointed at the road straight ahead.

"Can't miss it. Only place there that's got any eats." Chester took Ray's dollar, tipped his cap to my mama and walked back to the filling station door. He picked at his teeth and watched them drive away. He dialed up the telephone, I noticed. Whoever this Mr. Johnson was, he'd probably know what Ray wanted even 'fore they got there. That's how small towns is. Everybody passes on what they hears, soon's they hear it.

Ray made arrangements with that Mr. Johnson man and got the key. Give him five whole dollars for the week. Ray told him he and Mama was making it a second honeymoon and didn't want no one to know they was there and could he keep it a secret. Mr. Johnson said sure enough, be happy to. He come outside and said howdy to Mama. He had bad arthritis. He was crippled up more than MeeMaw ever was. If he took hisself a good look at Mama, he'd know they weren't on no honeymoon—second, third, or whatever—by the 'spression on her face.

When they got up to the cabin, Ray had to build a fire to keep them warm. It can get right cold in them Georgia mountains come sundown. Once Ray and Mama got settled, I started wondering what was going on with Melvin and Lexie and Mz. Hawkins and everybody back home. I found out that when I closed my eyes I got to the place where they was; simple as that. Nothing to it! I could hear 'em and see 'em and everything. This being no longer in the regular world weren't *all* bad. It was magical.

Aunt Lexie was beside herself when she got over to our trailer and found supper all ready and Mama nowhere in sight. Uncle Melvin said to hang on to her britches, that something must of come up and they'd find out directly; just to have a little patience. I think Aunt Lexie was one a' them kinds of people that can tell when something's wrong for sure, and she was fretting up a storm.

Sure enough, Sheriff Dooley and his deputy man come up to the trailer and talked with Melvin in real quiet tones and kept looking over at Lexie as they was whispering. Lexie was sitting on one of our kitchen chairs, holding Irl on her lap, and Alice was sitting on the floor playing with a little cloth doll Lexie made her. Uncle Melvin kept saying real soft like, "Oh my God. Oh my God." They might of been telling him about the money. It weren't hid all that good and Ray, he didn't take time to look for it at all when he hightailed it out of the woods. They probably found it by now. And they might could of been telling Melvin 'bout me if'n they seen my body floating along the river in Roseflower Creek. Could be, 'cause Uncle Melvin looked awful in the face and had to go set hisself down on the sofa.

"Lexie, honey, come here," he said. "Sheriff, can you take the kids on outside?"

"Melvin, what is it? What is it?" Lexie asked. She walked on over to Melvin, but she was looking up at the sheriff as she was doing it. He weren't saying anything. He just stood there and his deputy stood next to him by the door of our trailer. The sheriff said, "Who'd like to blow that siren in my car?" Irl went stumbling towards the door in his leg braces.

"I wanna do it!" he said. Alice got up, run over to the sofa and climbed into Lexie's lap. When the sheriff tried to take her she wouldn't have no part of it.

"It's okay. It's okay," Lexie said. "Let her stay with me, Melvin," she said. "They're scaring her." Melvin nodded at the sheriff.

"Darlin'," Melvin said. He pulled Lexie close to him and put his arm around her shoulder. He patted the back of Alice's blonde curls.

"They found Lori Jean floatin' in the creek, honey . . ."

"Hhuuuuuuuuhhhh . . ." Aunt Lexie started to shriek like a chicken done seen a fox in the hen house. Alice started crying, too, but I don't think she knew what she was crying for. She was just fussin' 'cause Lexie was making them scary noises.

"Lexie, honey, listen to me. Listen," Melvin said and put his hand across her mouth.

"They think Ray done it and . . ." Lexie kept shaking her head side to side and moaning like she didn't want to believe any of it.

". . . and they found some that payroll money, you know what was taken from the mill. They think he and Nadine done run off with the rest a' it. . . ."

"Noooooooo!" Lexie jumped up.

"Nadine wouldn't a' done that! I know Nadine wouldn't . . ."

Alice was screaming and hanging on to Lexie with all her might. Melvin looked up at the deputy.

"Would you take my family home?" he said. "And stop by Mz. Hawkins's and get her to come be with Lexie and the kids?" The deputy nodded. He come over to Lexie and took her gently by the arm.

"Come with us, Mz. Pruitt. This ain't no place to be right now," he said. Lexie looked at the table with all the food spread out. She spotted the birthday cake sitting on the counter and started to rock her body back and forth with Alice in her arms.

"Oh, what's goin' on? Oh God, what's goin' on?" Lexie cried out. Melvin took her by the shoulders and walked her out the door. He put both his arms around her. She leaned her head into his chest.

"Oh, Melvin," she said, "tell me it ain't so. Tell me our little Lori Jean's okay. Please . . ." Melvin shook his head.

"Oh, please, Melvin . . . ," Lexie said.

"You go on home now. I'm goin' with the deputies, Lexie. I got to help bring Ray in. I got to do this." Lexie started crying really hard. Her mouth was all twisted up and horrible sounds was coming from it. All the while she was bouncing Alice on her hip and patting her back trying to get her to stop crying and she was just a'wailing away herself. I knew she loved me and was crying over me and it hurt me to see her that way. I knew she didn't care whether Ray took that money and was in trouble. She never much trusted him to do much good anyway. So it had to be me being gone that was troubling her so. I wanted to tell her I was fine and not to worry none, but no matter how hard I tried to she just didn't hear me.

"Aunt Lexie, I'm just fine. Just fine. Don't be sad, hear?" But she just kept carrying on. It was real sorrowful it was. She done had so much sadness this past year, I just hated to be part of any more. Darn that no-good Ray for killing me. Now look what he done. He made Lexie hurt something awful and here my mama ain't even found out yet. He was gonna make her plumb awful sad, too.

The deputy stopped and picked up Mz. Hawkins 'fore he took Lexie home. Maybelle rattled on and on about what happened.

"And when Lori Jean told me she found that money, well you can imagine my horror. And the danger that girl must of been in. Why, they killed her to keep her quiet over that money. Now, I tried to keep her at my house. I begged her to stay with me, but she wouldn't have any part of it. Why, I told her, 'Now, Lori Jean,' I says, 'we're gonna call the authorities and let them handle this,' but no, she run off and . . ." The deputy leaned over towards her. Maybelle, she was sitting in the front seat of the squad car; Lexie and the kids was in the back.

"Mz. Hawkins, I don't think you ought to be carryin' on just now. This woman's been through a lot today . . ."

"Oh, my, yes . . . ," Maybelle said. "Well, Lexie, how's Little Irl's legs coming along?" Maybelle jumped from one thing to another. Prattled on and on. I don't think she got it that Lexie wasn't in no talking mood just then.

After that deputy dropped 'em off, he joined up with the sheriff over at the jailhouse. They was rounding up everybody to go hunting for Ray. It was a posse for sure. And they was acting like my mama was a criminal to be on the watch for, too.

"This is the only photo we got a' the suspects," the sheriff said. "It was taken the day they was married, but it's only been a couple a' years so they pretty much look the same. Look it over good." It was that nice picture Mr. Hawkins took of them at the reception. The one I liked the best. The one my mama looked so special on. If them men looked it over good like they was supposed to, they sure enough could tell she weren't no criminal. I noticed they each took their time when their turn come to look at the picture, so I wasn't worried none about that. I was worried over my mama and how she'd feel when she found out I wasn't coming up to be with them after all.

The sheriff swore the posse in, including Uncle Melvin, and they climbed into a passel a' vehicles and took off following the sheriff's squad car. He was headed in the right direction and I wondered how he knew which way Ray went. Then I remembered all the rain we'd had and how that dirt road out by our place showed the tracks of his truck at the end of the road. You could still see where Ray turned off to the right heading towards Sugarville.

I figured it was only a matter of time 'fore they found them and brought them in. It would be a relief to my mama. She still probably thought I was okay and would want to get home to me. And she weren't one to leave a mess, and I knowed she was thinking about all that food sitting out on the table spoiling and stinking up our trailer.

When I went back to the cabin where they was, Ray was rummaging around in the cupboards to see what was left on the shelves for them to eat. There was one can of beans and a can of corn and some beef jerky. He had Mama heat up the beans and corn and they ate the jerky right from the package. It sure wasn't like the birthday supper Mama spent so much time cooking. She didn't seem to be concerned about that, though. Her face had dark creases in it; deeper worry lines than I ever seen on her face a'fore.

"Ray, what's goin' on? Why won't you tell me?" she asked.

Ray swallowed down spoonfuls of the beans and finished

the corn Mama put on a tin plate for him. She ground some coffee beans she found in the cupboard and brewed it right over the fire in an old bent coffeepot she found in the pie safe.

"I will after we eat," he said. Mama poured him some of the coffee and drank the rest herself. She didn't touch any of the food she'd put on her plate. It was a white china plate with pink flowers and gold edges. It looked old and had chips along one edge, but still, it was real pretty and I wondered how it ended up at that old fishing shack.

"You gonna eat that?" Ray motioned at the corn and beans on the china plate. Mama shook her head no. Ray took his fork and dragged the plate over to him, ate what was on it and let out a belch.

Mama got up and started clearing the table just like she done at home. She pumped water into a kettle and set it on the stove to boil and washed the few dishes and put them back where she found them. Ray nosed around and found a bottle of corn liquor in the shed outside. He come back inside and poured hisself a glassful. Mama done something I *never* seen her do. She poured some of it in a glass for herself and took a big swallow. She swallowed hard and scrunched her eyes together when it went down. Didn't look like she liked it none too much, but she took another swallow just the same.

Ray lit a kerosene lamp and sat in a chair by the fire. Mama wrapped herself in a blanket she pulled off the bed and sat on the floor next to the hearth. Bits of burnt kindling snapped and popped. Sparks come shooting out ever' once in a while. There wasn't any screen covering the fire and I was sore afraid the sparks would catch hold of Mama and set her on fire. She didn't seem none to worried. She just burrowed in closer.

"Nadine, I ain't done right by you, girl," Ray said. Mama looked over in his direction.

"I want ya' to know I had every intention that day we got married that things was gonna be different." Mama kept staring at him.

"And I know mostly they haven't been, 'ceptin' for a short time after the fire." Mama just sat there nodding her head.

"And I ain't forgot what you done for me, gettin' me back on my feet. Ain't no one ever been better to me in my whole life than you, Nadine. No one, not even my mama. God knows she tried, but my pa never let her get near me." Ray took a big swig of that corn liquor.

"See, Nadine, all my life I just ain't been able to be what I was supposed to be. It's like . . . it's like no matter what chance I get I . . . these things inside me, these demon things, they . . ." Ray took another big swallow of that white lightning.

"Nadine, I done somethin' so terrible . . . there's no way you're gonna . . . there's no way I kin . . . see, what I done, well, I ain't gonna be able to make it right. It's just . . . I want you ta' know . . . I've tried to be . . . I've tried . . ." Ray took another swallow and then *he* done something I ain't never seen *him* do before. He started crying. Not hollering crying like he did at the creek that day he saw I wan't breathing no more, but crying like you do when your heart's plumb broke apart. Crying like I cried when I lost Carolee. Crying like Mama and me did when we found MeeMaw dead in her bed that winter when I was seven. He started crying like that and just couldn't stop.

And I watched and I watched and something happened to me inside. So deep inside I felt it run through every part of me. Every bit of hate and anger and bitterness I had for that man just sprang right out of my chest. And when I looked at Ray, he weren't a man no more. He was a little boy, six or seven maybe, and he was crying and his nose was all bloody and he was begging his pa to stop whipping him. And here I was no longer in that world and I was crying right along with him and begging his pa to stop hurting him.

"Please, Mr. Pruitt," I said. "Don't hurt Ray no more. He's just a little boy. He needs your love. Little children needs it to grow and be right in the head when they's grown up. He needs it so he can be the man he's supposed to be." I looked over at Ray and he was still a little boy, only now he was about eight or nine and he'd been whipped with a cat-o'-nine-tails and couldn't get to the shed, and he was peeing all over his bed.

"Can you hear me, Mr. Pruitt?" I said. "See what you done? Ray can't get to the shed. He's done peed all over his covers." And I looked up and Ray was rolling those covers into a ball and trying to hide them under the bed and his daddy was putting his overhauls on in another room and he come in and found Ray rolling up those smelly covers and he started smacking little Ray so hard he went flying into the wall. Now his face was all bloody. Ray rubbed it with the back of his hand, but before he could check to see how bad he was bleeding, Mr. Pruitt punched him right in the face with his fist. "Please, Pa," Ray said. But his pa never listened. He just beat Ray 'til he couldn't stand. I looked closer and I saw Ray's mama walk to another room and sit down in a rocking chair. She rocked and rocked. All the time little Ray was being beat she rocked and rocked. What would make a mama just sit and rock when that was going on? Then I looked into Ray's mama's eyes while she sat in that rocking chair and I seen them same beatings come down on her body, only she was a much younger woman then, real pretty with long dark curls. Ray was crawling at her feet and Melvin was in a highchair. Her tummy was all swelled up with another baby growing inside. I seen Mr. Pruitt come at her with his fists. And he hit her 'til she fell down. Then he picked her up, carried her outside, and throwed her down the cellar steps. I looked into that black hole of a cellar and heard her scream all the way to the bottom. The next time I looked, her eyes was black and her tummy wasn't swollen up with a baby no more.

And then I knowed how a mama could sit rocking in a chair when horrible things was happening. A mama like that had no life left in her. On the outside she was alive, but inside she was dead. All that was left was fear. She was plumb full of it. She had no sign of happiness about her. She had no hope. It was like things was never gonna be different. And worse, she knew it. I looked again. Ray was still crying. He was still a young boy. Now maybe ten or eleven. It was dark. So dark I had trouble making out his outline in the room. His daddy had him bent over on the bed and I knowed he was doing to him what Uncle Melvin told me their pa done to Ray for years. Ray was begging his pa to stop. He was screaming.

"Don't, Daddy! Oh, please, please don't! It hurts, Daddy! It hurts!" Ray said, and he was crying so hard. Ray's pa just kept smacking his man part into Ray's butt, all the while pushing the back of Ray's head into the covers.

"Mr. Pruitt!" I yelled. "Stop it! Stop it! Don't ya' see what this done to yer boy? Ya' done broke Ray up good inside so he can't never be well!"

I was tugging on Mr. Pruitt as hard as I could, but I couldn't feel his arm and I'm sure he couldn't feel mine. There weren't nothing I could do. I knowed I wasn't really there. It was a glimpse of Ray's memories I was seeing, his nightmares, them ones that haunted him his whole life.

"Don't ya' see what Ray coulda been?" I asked. "Don't ya'?" But even if he did, it was too late. Wherever Mr. Pruitt was now, his being sorry wasn't gonna change it. But knowing what Ray been through could change us. In those minutes that I saw Ray's past, I forgive him for everything he ever done bad, right there on the spot.

"It's okay, Ray," I called out. "It's okay. Don't cry no more. Don't blame yourself none. I know you didn't mean it. I know deep in your heart you wanted to live up to being what you coulda been. You just didn't have the right chance is all. You didn't have the right materials to do it with, just like Melvin said. I don't hold it against you, Ray. I don't. And I forgive you, Ray! I forgive you! I do! Don't cry!" But he couldn't hear me. He just kept crying.

It felt so good forgiving Ray. I found out when I didn't have that anger and hatred for him inside me it left a light, happy feeling in its place, a feeling that everything would work out in the end no matter what I tried to do. That the world and the peoples in it and the way they behaved wasn't my fault. I didn't have to take care of them no more. It weren't my fault my real daddy took off. It weren't Mama's fault Ray was mean. It weren't anyone's fault babies died and grandmas got sick. It was all part of life. Some parts is good, somes is not. Once I forgive Ray I got me peace like I never had me before. I knew then we'd been a family all along. A family with hurts and wounds and nightmares maybe, but still a family. A family with good parts and sad parts. A family with some happy times, too. Sure enough, we had some of those. I guess we had it all. And now I had me an understanding that life is just that way. That it's best we take what it gives us and accept it. So that's what I done. I forgived and I accepted.

I wanted my mama to feel peace and understanding, to have them warm feelings inside her I had in me. I wanted her to have this lightness in her heart I now had in mine. And for sure I wanted her to have it before Ray told her what happened to me.

"Dear Lord," I prayed, "I hope you can hear me extra good 'cause I think I'm pretty close by. Please help my mama forgive Ray for what he done. That's all I ask. Just help my mama forgive him. 'Cause then, no matter what happens, I know she'll be okay."

chapter twenty-one

Ray still hadn't told Mama what he done to me. He drunk too much that night he did all that crying in the cabin and passed out. Mama left him there right in that chair next to the fire and climbed in the bed in the back of the cabin. He was too heavy for Mama to move, but even if he weren't I don't think she would of helped him none. She looked all over for the keys to the truck. They was in his jean pocket, but Ray was slumped over half on his side and she couldn't get to 'em. I think she would of took off and left him there if she could of got those keys. She kept trying, but finally give up when Ray come awake for a bit and pushed at her.

"Leave me be," he said. So that's what she done. She didn't even cover him up with a blanket, and there was an extra one folded up on the bed even. That's how mad she was at him for dragging them off and not telling her what was going on.

In the morning they was mighty hungry. There weren't nothing for them to eat. Ray already eat up what little food they found in the pantry the night before.

"Ray, we gotta get ourselves some groceries, unless you're fixin' to starve us to death, too," Mama said when he woke up.

"Let's just move on to the next town. We'll get somethin' to eat there," he said.

"I'm not goin' any farther, Ray, 'til you tell me what's goin' on," Mama said. "You can beat me silly. Go ahead. I'm stayin' right here 'til you tell me in God's name what we're doin' traipsin' cross the country like outlaws." Mama sat at the table with her arms crossed real tight against her chest. If'n she was ever gonna pick a time to go against him this was a good one. Ray was pretty sick from that corn liquor he drunk so much of. When Mama said she weren't going any farther, Ray got up and headed towards her. He had a look in his eye like death and the devil was coming to call, but when he reached my mama he kept on going. He made it out the cabin door just in time, and threw up whatever was left of that corn liquor. When he finished he went out to the truck and got his rifle. It was the .22 Hornet he used to shoot varmints with.

"It's the only thing our pa ever give him," Uncle Melvin once said. "He didn't give him a thing to take into this world and then leaves him a gun so he can take plenty outa it. Go figure."

Ray and Uncle Melvin hunted rabbits and squirrels mostly. We ate 'em, too. Mama could fix 'em up mighty tasty. One day they come home after all the bullets was gone.

"We ain't got a thing to show for our efforts today, Lori Jean," Uncle Melvin said. "I figure we fired ten rounds 'fore we run out."

"Ten rounds each?" I said.

"Yep. What do you think?"

"I think there's been some mighty poor shootin'," I said.

I sure hoped Ray hadn't gotten any better with his aim. He reached under the front seat of the truck and pulled out two handguns. Where he got those I have no idea. I ain't never seen 'em before. He had two boxes of bullets he gathered up with the guns and went on back to the cabin. Mama was still sitting there waiting on him.

"You want to hole up here," he said, "suit me fine."

"Well, that's good," Mama said, " 'cause I ain't movin' 'til I know why I is."

"I done killed someone, Nadine. The law's after me by now for sure. Reckon we'll just wait on 'em, then."

"Oh, my God!" Mama said. "Who'd you kill?"

"I stole that payroll money, too."

"The payroll money? You mean that money from the mill?"

"That be it."

"Oh, Ray . . ."

"We'd be outa here, too, if I had my hands . . ." Ray slammed his fist down hard on the table.

"Who'd you kill, Ray? Paper didn't say nothin' 'bout nobody gettin' killed," Mama said.

"That come later. It weren't intentional," Ray said. Mama eyed the guns Ray was loading.

"And I s'pose the rest a' the killin' you plan on doin' is?"

"A man's gotta do what a man's gotta do."

"Well, I want no part a' this," Mama said. She got up from the table and went to get what little she brought with 'em.

"Sit down, Nadine!" Ray aimed the pistol right at her backside and cocked the trigger. Mama spun around.

"You gonna shoot me, Ray?"

"If I have to," he said.

"Go ahead, then," Mama said. "Seems you killed a man, might as well kill me dead, too. We ain't got no life to go back to anyway."

"What about Lori Jean. You thought about her?" Ray said, and that weren't playing fair even. He knew Mama didn't have to worry none about me no more.

"Lori Jean . . . ," Mama said. "Oh, sweet Jesus, what's gonna happen to Lori Jean?"

"Well, there you go, you got lots to go back to," Ray said. "Now sit yourself down, woman."

I knew from checking on Melvin and the sheriff's men that if Ray and Mama didn't move on they'd be caught for sure real soon. The posse was close by. They'd made it on up to that little town of McCoy where Ray got gas the day before. The sheriff showed that nice fella Chester the picture of Mama and Ray. Chester told the sheriff about George Johnson's place where he reckoned they'd be. One of the deputies went and got Mr. Johnson from the café so he could direct them to his fishing cabin.

"Well, I'll be," he said. "I knew somethin' wasn't right about that fella. I kin spot a bad one." He climbed into the deputy's car all excited. If'n his arthritis was causing him pain he sure didn't show it. They joined up with the others, and Mr. Johnson, he got in the sheriff's car. He sat right up at the edge of the seat and give the sheriff a shortcut to the cabin. Melvin's truck was right behind the sheriff's. Burt Peters was riding with him and had a shotgun in his hand.

All the other cars and trucks got in line and took off following. Must of been twenty of them. It was something to see.

It didn't take 'em long to get to the cabin. The sheriff had everyone park their cars at the bottom of the hollow and climb the banks up to the top on foot. He fanned them all out in a circle and when they got up to the edge of the landing everyone got down on their bellys and inched towards the fishing shack where Ray and Mama was.

Before they climbed up there, the sheriff had Burt Peters wait by the squad car with Mr. Johnson. He didn't want that old man to get hisself hurt none.

"This man done killed his own little girl. Beat her to death," he said. He was talking about me. I weren't really Ray's girl, but guess they took it like I was, him being married to my mama.

"He'd plug a hole in you, Mr. Johnson, soon as look at you," the sheriff said. "You stay on down here, now. No tellin' what's gonna happen up there." So, Mr. Johnson done like he said. And Burt Peters stayed with him.

"Now, Sheriff, let me talk to him when we get up there," Melvin said. "He'll listen to me." Sheriff Dooley nodded his head.

All told there was about forty men in the posse, so the cabin was surrounded but good. Ray didn't have no choice but to come out with his hands up. And that's just what the sheriff yelled for him to do.

"Ray Pruitt!" he called out. "We know you're in there. We've got you surrounded." Ray grabbed his rifle off the table and run over to the window. Sure enough, he could see men was everywhere.

"Come out with your hands up! The both a' you!" the sheriff said. Ray busted a hole in the window glass and fired a round at the sheriff. That shot went right over the sheriff's head. Missed him good. Sheriff Dooley dropped to the ground to get hisself out of the line of fire and the rest of the posse did the same. Now everyone was back on their bellys again.

Ray fired the rifle again and it hit the tree right next to where the sheriff was crouched down. Him and his men started firing back. Melvin was yelling, "Hold yore fire! Let me talk to him." Nobody listened. They just peppered that cabin with bullets, they did.

Mama hit the floor. Ray raised the rifle and fired it again, but it jammed up. It did that a lot when they was hunting varmints, too. Ray crawled over to the table and grabbed hold of the pistol, the big one with the long barrel. He tucked the other gun, the smaller one, into his belt and gathered the boxes of bullets in the crook of his arm and made his way back to the window.

"Are you plumb crazy, Ray?" Mama said. "That's Sheriff Dooley out there. You need to give yourself up 'fore you get us both killed."

"Suit yourself, Nadine," he said. "I'm done givin'. Now, I'm gonna start takin'." Ray fired the rounds in the gun he loaded up earlier. This time he hit a deputy right in the chest. The deputy fell backwards and grabbed the front of hisself. Blood was just pouring out of him. He looked down and his hands was covered in it. That poor man didn't say a word. He just slumped over on the ground and closed his eyes. I think he was dead for sure. One of the other men made it over to him and dragged him to the woods.

Melvin stood off to the side in a small clearing. He took his cap off and slammed it hard against his overhauls. He put his other hand on top of his head and pulled it down towards his chin. He squeezed his eyes like he was trying to shut out the noise. Then he put his cap back on and looked around at all the men firing their rifles.

"Let me talk to him, Sheriff!" he yelled. "Let me talk to him for chrissakes!" The sheriff didn't answer him. The posse man that dragged the injured man into the woods called out, "He's dead, Sheriff."

"They done killed Bernie Jacobs!" he yelled. So, I was right. Ray killed that deputy man dead, all right. Now he was really in trouble. He'd get the 'lectric chair for sure. Melvin run over to the spot where that Bernie guy was laying and put his ear next to his face. He held it there for a long time. When Melvin looked up, he had one hand over his eyes and I seen his shoulders shaking theirselves up and down. He patted the man's chest nice like. Then he got up and punched a tree that was standing next to him 'til his hand got bloody.

All the men there, except Melvin, was firing their guns 'til they was empty. Then they loaded up and fired again. Bullets was flying into that cabin from all directions. Mama screamed, "I'm comin' out! I'm comin' out!" She started for the cabin door. It had more holes in it than that bad-tasting cheese MeeMaw used to like so much. Before she even got halfway there, a bullet come whizzing though the windowpane and hit Ray in his right shoulder. The gun he was shooting went flying across the room towards Mama. He let out a howl and grabbed his arm.

"Jesus Christ almighty!" Ray yelled. "I caught one in the shoulder." He took his belt off and started to wrap it tight around the top part of his arm. The little gun he had shoved in the waistband of his jeans dropped out on the floor. He tried to pick it up with his right hand, but his arm wasn't working good no more. He used his left hand instead. Ray couldn't hardly shoot straight with his regular firing hand. Now he was fixing to shoot left-handed. It was good news for the deputies.

They was closing in on the cabin. Then everything got real quiet. The sheriff was motioning all the men to hold their fire.

"Nadine Pruitt, you need to give yourself up," he said. "Do right by your little girl." Mama was on the floor sobbing. I don't know if she heard him. I think she was in shock or something 'cause she didn't move no closer to the cabin door or nothing, and just minutes before when them bullets was flying all around her she said she was coming out.

"Nadine? You hear me? This is Sheriff Dooley. You come

out with your hands up. I'll personally see to it you can bury your little girl 'fore we lock you up. You hear me?"

When Mama heard what the sheriff said she got up on her knees and looked over at Ray, but she didn't say a word. She didn't ask any questions and she didn't answer any of the sheriff's, neither. There was a look on her face hard to describe. It was a look that said I don't need to ask no questions 'cause now I got me plenty of answers. It was a look I ain't seen on my mama's face ever before. It was a mighty scary look, and I wanted her to wash it off 'fore it froze in place, so her face could be soft like I remembered it all them nights she tucked me in. Mama's lips was pressed tight together, and her eyes was ever' bit as spooky as Darla Faye's cat—and a mighty scary cat he was. He could stare ya' down and make ya' run. Mama stared at Ray like that, only Ray didn't run. She stared at him like she could see into his soul, like she could see every dirty deed he ever done and the ones he was still fixing to do. It give me the goosey bumps.

"Ray Pruitt!" the sheriff called out. "We found Lori Jean in the creek bed. We know what you done to her." The sheriff, he motioned for his men to come in closer to the cabin. He was moving in along with them. Melvin was right beside him. The men had their guns ready, 'cepting Melvin. He didn't have one.

"Wait, let me talk to him!" Uncle Melvin said. The sheriff didn't pay him no mind.

"Don't make this no harder on yourself," Sheriff Dooley called out. "You two come on out now with your hands up. It's the last time we're gonna ask you." Ray didn't answer none. And Mama didn't say nothing, either. It got so quiet you could hear the squirrels rustling in the trees, and somewhere nearby a little bird was chirping. The sheriff motioned for everyone to keep moving in. Inside the cabin Ray was trying to get a look-see out the window to find out what was going on. I think after all that gunfire the stillness spooked him good.

"You killed her, didn't you?" Mama said. "Lori Jean found that money. That's what was in that sack you kept pestering her about." Ray didn't say nothing. He kept looking out that window. I think he spotted one of the men behind a tree just a stone's throw away. Ray had the small gun in his left hand and he was aiming it out the window. He had his finger on the trigger. His regular firing arm was just hanging down by his side and blood was dripping all over the cabin floor.

"She told you it burned up in the fire and you didn't believe her, and when she wouldn't give it to you, you killed her," Mama said. She about figured most of it out. She sure did.

"You killed my Lori Jean. Now you killed yourself a deputy," Mama said. "But you ain't gonna kill nobody else, not today, not ever." Mama picked up the gun laying next to her on the floor, that very gun Ray killed that deputy with, the one they shot right out of his hand. She was fixing to shoot Ray. I seen it in her eyes. Ray didn't notice. He was still pointing that little pistol out the window.

"Mama," I called to her. "Don't do it, Mama! It's okay he killed me. He didn't mean it. He got a sickness in him, Mama," I said. Mama aimed the gun.

"Mama! Don't you see? Killin' Ray won't fix nothin'," I said, hoping somehow she'd hear me.

"I know yore plumb mad at him for what he done to me and plenty mad, too, for all the mean things he done to you, but, Mama, you gotta understand where all that meanness come from." Mama had her finger on the trigger. She cocked the gun.

"Mama," I said, "all that meanness in Ray, he just passed on to us what got passed on to him. I figured it out. That's how it works!" I don't think Mama heard me none. I don't think she heard nothing right then but maybe some voice in her head.

"Ray Pruitt," Mama said. He looked over at Mama and seen the gun in her hand.

"Give me that thing, Nadine," he said, "'fore you hurt yourself." Boy, he sure couldn't judge no situation real good. Couldn't he see Mama meant business? He should of been begging her forgiveness 'stead of giving her orders.

"This is for Lori Jean," Mama said, and she fired that gun straight at Ray. It hit him right in the middle of his chest. He sucked in his breath and fell backwards on the floor. His mouth hung open and his eyes stared right at her. I think he was having trouble believing she just shot him 'cause his face sure looked confused. The pistol fell out of his hand. He reached towards Mama like for her to help him.

"Nadine," he said. "Nadine." It come out of his chest all raspy like and bubbles of blood come out his mouth with it.

"This one's for that deputy," Mama said and fired again. That bullet hit Ray in the belly. He made some bad awful noises then.

"Help me, Nadine," he said. "I'm hurt bad." And he sure was. I figured he had no chance of making it now, and I hoped it ended soon. I didn't want to see him dead, but I surely didn't want to hear him suffering no longer. I was fixing to tell Mama it was a crying shame, she best end Ray's suffering, but I didn't get a chance to.

"And this one's for me," Mama said. She fired one more shot. It hit him right between the eyes. I didn't know Mama could shoot so good. Ray didn't move after that. She killed him dead.

The sheriff heard all the firing inside the cabin and made a run for the door. Melvin was still right behind him. The rest of the men come running after them. A shot rang out. One of them posse men was running too fast. He tripped over a log and fired his gun without meaning to. And that bullet, it did the worst thing it could of done. It headed right towards the first body it come to. Sheriff Dooley was at the cabin door by then, but he never even turned around when that bullet got fired; he just yelled, "Hold yore fire, you idiots!" Then he took his foot the size a' Texas and kicked the cabin door clean off its hinges. But Uncle Melvin, he wasn't behind the sheriff no more. That bullet got fired by accident—well—the first body it come to was his. He was sprawled face-down in the dirt with a big hole shot clean through him. Liked to took my breath away, and it already been took.

chapter twenty-two

The sheriff found my mama curled up next to Ray with her arms wrapped around him. She done killed him and now she was hugging on him. I think Mama lost the cookies in her head God give her, for sure. Any fool could see that; one a' them temporary 'sanity things or something.

I was real sorrowful over Mama killing Ray like that, but I was even more sorrowful when I realized she used that gun Ray shot and killed that deputy man with. Her finger marks was probably all over that gun by now. They might could think she killed that deputy, what with Ray not alive to tell them no different.

"Nadine Pruitt, you're under arrest," the sheriff said. They put handcuffs on her and took her back down the hill to the squad car where Mr. Johnson was. Mama didn't give 'em no trouble. She didn't even talk to them none. Didn't say one word. The sheriff told Burt Peters to take Mr. Johnson and fetch an ambulance quick like for Melvin and to get this coroner man to come see about Ray's body.

Two men helped Melvin over to a big tree and leaned him against it. He was hugging his shoulder. That Melvin were a tough one, I'm telling ya'. That bullet didn't even kill him dead and it sure shoulda. This doctor where they took him said Melvin had so many muscles high up on his back where the bullet hit, it saved his life. Seems the bullet got stuck in them muscle layers and didn't do much damage. Fancy that. Moving trailers probably saved Melvin's life for sure 'cause mostly that's where he got all them muscles from. Once they tended to Melvin at the cabin as best they could, they took him to a hospital in Dahlonega on the way back. That's where that doctor was said that stuff about Uncle Melvin's muscles.

Everyone else headed back to Decatur. When they got to the jailhouse, they give Mama a plain brown dress to put on and locked her in a cell all by herself. Come morning I stood next to Mama and watched her cry on the newspaper the sheriff man brought to her cell. They had a picture of me on the front page. Fancy that. And that paper had this article all writ up nice, telling folks what happened. It was a real good story. It told how Mz. Hawkins found out about the money and how she called the authorities and they come looking for me to where they figured I'd run off to and then how they found bits of the payroll money here and there around the outhouse. It said they found me at the edge of the creek bed. I'd floated right over to some logs and my hair got stuck in some branches, so thankfully, I didn't get very far, they said. They wrote my arm was busted, my spleen was teared, my intestines was split, and my windpipe was broken, too. That part upset my mama so bad she asked the deputy man to come and take the newspaper away. But that wasn't what upset me the most. I wasn't even mad when it said Mz. Hawkins was getting all the reward money. I was real bad upset about the last part; the part where Sheriff Dooley give this reporter man an interview or something. They couldn't fit all of it on the page and that was good, but I knowed what he said. I was right next to him when he said it.

"Can you tell us what happened, Sheriff?" that reporter fella asked him.

"We got a call from Mz. Maybelle Hawkins a' Roseflower Creek yesterday mornin'. Told us she had information as to who took the payroll money," the sheriff said.

"Go on."

"Well, we found some a' the money in the vacinity, and we found the young'un of the guy who done it dead in the creek." Sheriff Dooley wiped the sweat from his face with his hankie.

"And the child's name?" the reporter asked.

"That'd be Lori Jean Dodson, age ten," the sheriff read from his notes, which was mighty peculiar. He knowed who I was. Been knowing me my whole life. That Sheriff Dooley, he was showing hisself off for sure, I'm telling ya'.

"What about the girl's parents?" The reporter was writing everything down the sheriff said.

"Well, that's just it. They was long gone and so was the rest a' the money. At least at the time, we thought it was."

"And you figured they killed their own kid before they took off?"

"Dang right. People do right strange things for money. Far as we can figure that kid was tellin' on them. Told Mz. Hawkins all about it. Asked for help in turning the money in. We figure her ma and pa killed her to hush her up."

"And then . . ."

"And then, we tracked 'em all the way to Sugarville. They was holed up in the mountains in a fishin' cabin. That's where we found 'em, the both a' them, Nadine and Ray Pruitt, guns drawn, ready for a fight."

"The Pruitts fired first?"

"Darned tootin' they did. We give 'em fair warning to come out. And that's when Nadine Pruitt killed Deputy Bernie

Jacobs. Then she shot and killed her husband before attemptin' to turn the gun on herself," the sheriff said. That was all lies, and here that newspaperman done put it in the paper like it were facts in the Bible.

"Wait a minute," the reporter said. "Pruitt? I thought you said the kid's name was Dodson."

"I did. Ray Pruitt weren't the child's natural father. But it's my understanding he's 'bout the only pa she ever knew."

"Did they have the money with them when you caught up to them?"

"Matter of fact, they didn't," the sheriff said. "We located it this morning; found it in the hollow of an old tree in the woods near their property."

"Seems rather peculiar they didn't bother to take it with them, don't you think?" the reporter said.

"We're workin' on that. Got a few theories," the sheriff said.

"When's the trial?" the reporter asked.

"Near as I been told, next week," Sheriff Dooley said.

"You figure she'll get the electric chair?"

"No, I don't figure she'll get the chair," the sheriff said, "I *guarantee* you she'll get the chair. That be a fact and you can print it." Sheriff Dooley tipped his hat and left after posing for a picture. That newspaper, when it come out, had big black letters printed at the top of the first page: LOCAL SHERIFF CRACKS PAYROLL ROBBERY. TAKES KILLER INTO CUSTODY.

It was real sorrowful, it was. Everybody done tried my mama and found her guilty already. What kind of fair trial is that? I knowed then Mama was gonna have to set every one a' them lawmen fellas down and tell 'em exactly what happened out there; there weren't no if's, and's, or but's about it. She had to save herself. But that wasn't exactly the way it worked out 'cause Mama still weren't talking to nobody.

chapter twenty-three

The folks at the jail was real nice to Mama. They give her this attorney man to help her. He was a public offender, I think they said. He was free and a real nice man. He come to see Mama right away. He talked in a soft voice to her and wore his Sunday go-to-church suit even. He had suspenders and a little bow tie. He looked real special and I figured the jury would listen to him good. His words come out in nice sentences, and even though he used these big words they sounded right good when he said 'em. His name was Elmer Addicus Howard, but he weren't no relation to my meemaw, Mavis Howard. The judge called him Counselor, which didn't make no sense. How'd he get hisself a nickname Counselor from Elmer Addicus?

He give this opening statement and said my mama was a victim herself of Ray Pruitt, and he would present his case accordingly. This other attorney fella wasn't nice to my mama at all. He sat at this other table a little ways over from Elmer Addicus and he said bad things about Mama to the jury, and he didn't even know her. He said she was a mother with no feelings at all, a woman he said who allowed her own daughter to be killed so the money her and her husband stole could remain a secret. He told them she was a woman who shot and killed Deputy Bernie Jacobs over that same money, a woman who in the end shot and killed her husband, too, when she realized they were surrounded; a woman who intended to then kill herself, but coward that she was, couldn't.

"That woman, Nadine Pruitt, sits before you now!" that attorney fella yelled out and pointed his finger at Mama.

"And that woman deserves your guilty verdict and a verdict of death in the electric chair. Thank you, ladies and gentlemen," he said, and then he sat down. His name was Lester Bartholomew the Third. So there was two more mens just like him somewhere, but they never showed up and I was real glad about that. Funny thing, though. This Bartholomew the Third guy, he had hisself the same nickname as Elmer Addicus Howard, Mama's attorney fella. Fancy that! The judge called Mr. Bartholomew Counselor, too. Isn't that something?

Mr. Bartholomew's daddy was a congressman, and some said he wanted to be governor and that's why he took the job he had of sending people to jail, so he could get a lot of people to vote for him some day. Which didn't make no sense, neither. All them people he sent to jail probably wouldn't vote for him. Other people said if he got my mama sent to the electric chair for what they said she done to Bernie Jacobs, he'd be elected for sure. Bernie Jacobs had hisself a wife and two little children. Mrs. Jacobs come to court every day and sat in the first row and cried a bunch whenever that lawyer man Mr. Bartholomew mentioned him during the trial. Folks in the jury seats always looked at her real sad like. I think they felt real sorry for her and I don't blame 'em. I did, too. She had two little children to take care of now, all by herself.

Some of them people that got to watch the trial felt bad for my mama, too. Said she was a good woman; got herself involved with the wrong man. Weren't that the truth. I wished them folks was on the jury, 'stead of on them benches watching. Maybelle come, too. She got to sit in the second row and never had to wait in line like the others. Sheriff Dooley had one his deputies take her to her seat 'fore they even let the others in. Probably on account Sheriff Dooley said it was her more than anyone cracked their case. Maybelle was looking real fine at the trial. Had her hair all done up nice and she wore a different dress every day, ones I never seen, so they was probably new for sure. And Maybelle must of put herself on a special diet or something 'cause she was losing weight like crazy. I could even see her waist, and I ain't never seen that before. Then one day she didn't come no more. People was buzzing all about. Said she was powerful sick; seeing a special doctor in Atlanta.

"You hear 'bout Maybelle?" Myrtle Soseby said during one them break times the judge give so people can refresh themselves. In truth, they mostly all went and relieved themselves in the rooms marked WOMEN or MEN in black letters on frosty glass windows.

"What about Maybelle?" Mz. Murphy and old Mz. Hattaway asked at the same time and crowded about Myrtle in a circle with the other ladies come in to do their business. Myrtle whispered a bunch of words I couldn't make out. Everybody gasped.

"Not sure what kind, but she's powerful sick from what I hear," Myrtle said.

"Probably got herself a terminal case of meanness," Mz. Murphy said. And somes the ladies laughed. Weren't that mean? 'Cause turns out it weren't meanness a'tall; it was the cancer! It was the kind that eat the bottom part of Maybelle's 'testines, keeped her poopy. Isn't that terrible? The doctors in Atlanta said there weren't nothin' much they could do for her, 'cept give her this operation, called a "colostummy" or something. Told her they had to sew a bag outside her stomach where she could do her business. Said it was the best they could do. It was real sorrowful. Maybelle's face turned as white as them lacy bloomers she liked to wear. I don't rightly blame her none. If that's the best them doctors could do, they must not of thunk on it too long 'cause who wants a poopy sack sticked right out on top of their tummy? But Maybelle said, "No use standin' there; let's git it over with," and she went and had herself that operation, seeing as it was the best they could do. She missed the rest of the trial.

All kinds of folks come to testify. Mr. Johnson drove over from Sugarville. Mr. Bartholomew asked him all kinds of questions on how he ended up letting Ray and Mama stay at his cabin. Mama's lawyer, Mr. Howard, got up and asked him a few questions, too.

"Good morning, Mr. Johnson. I'm Attorney Howard, representing the defendant, Mrs. Nadine Pruitt," he said.

"Mornin'," Mr. Johnson said back to him.

"Mr. Johnson, on the morning Ray Pruitt inquired of your cabin, did you get an opportunity to see Mrs. Pruitt?"

"I believe I did, yes sir," Mr. Johnson said.

"Would you be so kind as to tell the jury your first impression of Mrs. Pruitt?"

"My first impression?"

"Yes," Mr. Howard said.

"You mean what I was thinkin' the moment I first laid eyes on her?"

"Precisely," Mr. Howard answered.

"Well, I was thinkin' she had herself one fine pair a' legs."

The jury burst out laughing, they did, and Mr. Howard, he smiled, too.

"No doubt, Mrs. Pruitt is a fine-looking woman, Mr. Johnson, but that's not exactly what I was referring to," Mr. Howard said.

"Rather, can you tell us how you found her manner to be . . . was she overly quiet, did she appear frightened . . ."

"Objection, Your Honor, counsel's leading the witness," Attorney Bartholomew said.

"Sustained," the judge said.

"I'll rephrase the question, Your Honor," Mr. Howard said.

"Mr. Johnson, did Mrs. Pruitt appear to have a bruise on her—"

"Objection. Requires a conclusion. Mr. Johnson is not a physician," Mr. Bartholomew said.

"Overruled," the judge said.

"Your honor . . . ," Mr. Bartholomew said.

"Overruled!" the judge said and cracked his gavel. "I'm sure Mr. Johnson is perfectly capable of identifying a bruise without a medical degree. Sit down, Counselor!" The judge turned to Mr. Johnson sitting in the witness seat.

"You may answer the question."

"Wish I could," Mr. Johnson said. "Can't remember the dad-blame question." The judge smiled when he said that.

"Counselor, would you repeat the question, please?" the judge said. Guess he couldn't 'member it, neither.

"Did Mrs. Pruitt appear to have a bruise on her cheek?" Mr. Howard said.

"Well now, I can't say 'cause I don't rightly recall," Mr. Johnson said.

"Think back to that day, Mr. Johnson," Mr. Howard said. "Surely you can remember . . ."

"All's I remember is her havin' fine legs," Mr. Johnson said, "and I remember . . ."

"Yes . . . yes, Mr. Johnson . . . what?" Mr. Howard said.

"Well, I remember she had herself a right fine chest, too," Mr. Johnson answered. The jury and them other peoples there was back to laughing again. I think Mama even smiled a bit when he said that about her chest. I think I seen her mouth move a little.

I don't really think that was what Mr. Howard had in mind, though. He tried again and again to get Mr. Johnson to recall how scared my mama must of looked that morning.

"Mr. Howard, I don't remember nothing else," Mr. Johnson said, and he probably wasn't lying, either. He looked to be older than MeeMaw was when she died, and MeeMaw had trouble remembering things, too.

"Lori Jean," she told me once, "at my age, I've about done everything and seen everything. I just can't remember everything."

So Mr. Johnson was probably telling the truth. He just weren't much help to Mama's case. In fact, when Mr. Bartholomew questioned Mr. Johnson, he made it seem like everything was fine and dandy with my mama that morning.

I was waiting on that Chester fella to be called to the stand, that man that pumped gas for Ray at that filling station in McCoy. Mama was pleading at him with her eyes that day and he was glancing at that bruise she had on her cheek when Ray weren't looking. Now he was a young fella, not likely to forget what he seen that morning. He could help set things right. But he never showed up. Then I realized he wasn't invited. Mama was the only one would have known to tell Mr. Howard about him and she still weren't talking, not even to Mr. Howard. Mr. Howard even shared that with the jury, how

Mama wouldn't even defend herself she was so eat up with guilt by what she didn't know and by not knowing wasn't able to protect her daughter and save them both from the monster that Ray Pruitt was.

Uncle Melvin come and testified about Ray and I know the jury listened real good, what with Ray being his brother and all. Melvin, he was pretty much all better by then. And Lexie come and sat in the witness box and she told the jury folks about the nice birthday supper Mama fixed for me that was spread out on the table when they got to our trailer that night. I thought things was looking a bit better for Mama. If she would just get up in that witness chair and speak for herself, now that Uncle Melvin and Aunt Lexie come and told what a fine woman she was, she'd have a fighting chance, but she never said a word, not to Mr. Howard, not to the jury, not to Melvin or Lexie. She just sat and stared straight ahead.

On the last day of the trial more peoples than could fit wanted to get into the courthouse. Those that didn't get to wouldn't leave and clustered about the door like June bugs buzzing 'round a porch light. Mr. Bartholomew give his closing speech that day and he was so good he was like an actor in a stage play. He told that jury if they was going to sleep at night they best err on the side of justice and put this woman where she belonged. He said no amount of speculation by a well-intentioned attorney for the defense could erase what happened.

"Ladies and gentlemen," he said, "a little girl lies in her coffin, dead the very day she turned ten years old." He meant me, and I weren't in no coffin!

"A deputy lies cold in his grave, his widow sitting before you now weeping and broken," he said. Now that part was true. She was there crying like she done every day of the trial.

"Two toddlers face a future without their daddy, all because of this woman." He whirled around and pointed his finger directly at Mama.

"I ask you to bring justice to these precious victims, to bring closure to their wounds, to bring an end to the idea that this woman is innocent. I ask you to return a verdict of guilty, guilty as charged. Thank you, ladies and gentlemen, for doing your duty." He sat down.

When Mr. Howard give his closing statement all the ladies in the jury seats was crying. I don't think they heard what he had to say. The men was listening, but they had real stern looks on their faces. I don't think they much believed anything Mr. Howard was telling them.

The jury folks went to a little room behind the judge's bench to decide. They come out in less than an hour.

"Have you reached a verdict?" the judge asked.

The man that got voted to speak for them said, "We have, Your Honor." The judge told him to hand the verdict to his bailiff man. The jury man handed the bailiff fella a tiny little folded-up piece of paper. Fancy that! The answer to the whole rest of my mama's life was on that little piece of paper. The bailiff man brought it over to the judge. He unfolded it, read it to hisself and folded it back up and handed it back to the bailiff. The bailiff took it on back to the same man on the jury who'd handed it to him in the first place. It was worse than pass the hot potato. The judge told that man to read the verdict. Then the judge asked each and every one of the folks on that jury if that was their decision. They all said, "Yes, Your Honor; guilty, so sayeth we all."

So they found Mama guilty and the judge sentenced her to die in their old 'lectric chair and there weren't nothing I could do about it even. Hurt my heart something terrible. Mama was the first ladyfolk in Georgia ever to get that kind of sentence. The judge said the way things was going she probably wouldn't be the last.

"Nadine Pruitt," he said, "may God have mercy on your soul."

chapter twenty-four

Lexie fainted when the judge said Mama had to sit in that 'lectric chair 'til she was dead. He used some fancy words when he said it, but that's what he meant. The judge had them take Lexie to the sofa in his chambers and Melvin, he come to see about her. He was in bad shape but put on a good face for Lexie. They headed home and he give her this talk on how they had to get on with their life. The kids were counting on them.

"Sugarplum, I been thinkin'," he said, "we ought to head back to Alabama when this is . . . when . . . well, when . . . it's done." Lexie just nodded her head. They was in the Chevy. Lexie was driving on account of Melvin's shoulder still being in a sling.

"We ain't had much luck here, ya' know?" he said. Lexie shook her head in agreement with him.

"It's time we head home. I can always find some kind a' work to tide us over. Maybe try a little farmin' again." He reached over and patted Lexie's shoulder with his good arm.

"I want to go see Nadine," Lexie said.

"Now, honey, I don't want you to go upsettin' yourself . . ."

"I gotta say goodbye, Melvin. I have to. I can't rest 'til I do." Lexie started to sniffle.

"Honey, we're gonna get through this, you'll see," he said, and he patted her shoulder again.

"I know. It just hurts so bad, Melvin," Lexie said. "First Iris Anne, then Lori Jean. Now Nadine. I don't believe for one minute she had anything to do with any of it."

" 'Course she didn't," Uncle Melvin said. "But them authorities, they need theirselves a live person to pay for the crime and Nadine is it. I reckon if she wouldn't a' shot Ray, they wouldn't have bothered with her. Probably woulda made her a victim for sure. What with her bein' Lori Jean's mama and all."

"Then why'd she do it? Why'd she kill him?" Lexie asked. She grabbed a hankie out of her purse and blew her nose, but kept one hand on the wheel.

"I guess she wanted them both to pay, Lexie," Melvin said. "Him for doing it, and her for not being able to keep him from doing it."

"But she didn't know nothing about it," Lexie said. "I'm sure of it. How'd she figure she coulda kept him from doin' somethin' she had no way knowin' anything about?"

"Well that's just it, sugar," Melvin said. "She probably figured she should have known, that bein' a good mama demanded it."

"But she *was* a good mama."

"Better than good, Lexie," Melvin said. "The best. She give her life for Lori Jean. She just didn't get a chance to give it sooner is all, or Lori Jean would still be with us." Then Uncle Melvin, he cried. He did! He and Lexie—they both cried, all the way back to Roseflower Creek.

'Bout that time Maybelle got out of the hospital in Atlanta.

She looked like a 'tirely different person. Acted like one, too. She were a pretty thin lady now, had creases on her forehead like Mama sometimes did. And her mouth weren't so mean, looking no more. Matter of factly, it was a much nicer mouth, soft around the corners, and she smiled at folks when they passed by. Fancy that! And she kept her nose straight ahead when she walked, 'stead of pointed upwards like she used to. She still had her funny little bird legs, but now they matched her body better. Talk was, the kind of cancer Maybelle had herself would probably kill her dead; that what them doctors done for her with their crazy operation were just a temporary thing. Maybelle marched herself home and started visiting every church in Roseflower Creek, and she drove her big Oldsmobile to a whole bunch of others that weren't. Every one she stopped at, she asked folks to pray for her. And she give them all her money, week after week. Took every dollar in her pocketbook she had with her and put it in the collection basket. One of them mens who passed around the basket swung it by her row twice, acted like he didn't know he had. Maybelle found some more loose dollars at the bottom of her bag and give them, too. Word got out. They all wanted her to come. It were a church's lucky day when Maybelle showed up asking for prayers 'cause even though she'd give a whole lot of money away already, she had a passel more where that come from, I'm telling ya'. But no matter how many of them churches, went to, Maybelle got sicker and sicker. She ended up at the Glory Be, Church of Jehovah, Praise His Name, Bless My Soul, Amen Brethren AME Church in Roseflower Creek. That was Odell and Pearlie's church! It was the one all them nice colored folks went to; the very one Maybelle made fun of, that one she called a clapboard shack, said they did their jive jumpin' in. Ain't that something? There she was, jumping up and down right along with the rest of them, her on her funny little bird legs. She was whooping and hollering, praising Jesus' name and clapping her hands to the music. And mighty good music it was, I'm telling ya'. Been right nice to have that kind of music at our church when I was growing up. Maybelle was having the time of her life, and once she tried Odell and Pearlie's Glory Be Church, she stayed. She give them her money, week after week. They prayed over her and laid their hands on her. Still, Maybelle didn't get well. Looked like that cancer would kill her dead for sure. But Maybelle kept going, kept dancing, and kept giving.

All the while, Mama was locked up in her cell. For two months while the judge heard this appeal thing Mr. Howard brought to him, Mama stayed in that cell, walking back and forth, twisting her hands up in knots, not eating, not sleeping. I could be wrong, but I think she was worried they'd change their minds about 'lectricuting her. I don't think she wanted that to happen and the thought of it was making her sick. I guess she wanted to die. She was tore up with guilt and anger and regret. All them sorrowful things had her plumb eat up and dying 'fore she's even dying. It was a worse death than that old 'lectric chair even, 'cause it was a slow, suffocating death, one second at a time, it was.

"Mama?" I called to her. "Kin ya' hear me, kin ya'? Let it go, Mama! It'll just eat ya' alive right up to the end and there jist ain't no sense in goin' 'til you're goin'." I don't think she got my message, but she did get word her appeal got turned down and they set her death date three months away. She'd be gone 'fore Christmas.

Lexie come to see Mama for a goodbye visit. She packed some snacks for them to eat and the deputy lady was real nice, let her go right to Mama's cell. It was a few days before they were fixin' to take her on down to Jackson to wait on the execution date. Lexie and Mama spent the better part of the afternoon together. It was like a miracle. My mama was back to talking! She sounded like her old self again.

"Oh, my," Mama said and patted Lexie's tummy. "When's this one due?"

"Doc figures about four more months," Lexie said.

"Well, I guess I won't get to see this one then. . . ."

"Sure you will," Lexie said. "You'll have a bird's-eye view." Lexie hugged Mama good.

"You take care a' all those young'uns, ya' hear? You tell 'em their aunt Nadine's keepin' an eye on 'em for all eternity."

"I will," Lexie said and give her another hug. "I will, oh, I will," she said and didn't stop hugging Mama 'til the tears welling up in her eyes slipped back in place.

It was a real nice visit, it was. They talked about when they was little girls and how they met. They told old stories they thought they'd forgotten about. They was saying, "Remember this?" and "Remember that?" and had themselves a fine old time. Then they made a promise they'd see one 'nother again someday yonder. The warden lady come after that to tell Lexie it was time for her to go. After Lexie left, Mama seemed right peaceful. Guess everything was turning out the way she wanted. Before long, they brought in her dinner. Mama waited 'til they left 'fore she set down to eat it. Then she got on that bed was hooked onto the wall and for the first time in all them months since they put her there, she rested herself; slept like a baby, she sure enough did. It made my heart dance like it never done before, to see my mama rest herself like that. It felt so good I didn't much care if it never danced again.

chapter twenty-five

They found Mama in her cell the next morning. She was curled up under her covers, holding her tummy like it hurt something awful. She didn't have an ounce of breath left in her. Rat poison. It was in her mashed potatoes. Most of them was still on her plate, right next to the collard greens.

So's the State of Georgia never got to put my mama in their 'lectric chair, after all. I sure was happy about that. Rat poison didn't seem like a real nice way to go, neither, but at least she got to keep her hair. MeeMaw always said, "Lori Jean, be grateful for every little thing. They adds up." So I tried to think about that, her keeping her hair instead of what that poison probably done to her belly.

When Maybelle got word Mama was dead, she did something right special. She bought a grave spot right next to where Ray and Mama laid MeeMaw to rest. And then Maybelle did something even more special. She told the church people she wanted to buy the spot next to Mama, too, on account of me.

"A child needs to lie next to their mama," she said matter-of-factly. The church folks said that might could be, but there weren't no spot *next* to the spot she bought for Mama available.

Mr. Joshua Samuel Goose was there, waiting on Mrs. Goose.

"Well, can't you move him over one spot?" Maybelle asked. "It's real important," she told them. Well, they said, they weren't doubting that none, but if they moved him over one spot, where would Clara go? Clara, that was Mrs. Goose. She was pretty old and weren't too well herself.

"She might be needing that spot real soon," they said.

"Well, she ain't never got on with that ornery old man while he was alive," Maybelle said. "What makes you think she wants to lie next to him for all eternity?" Church folks wouldn't budge. Said it weren't their place to ask and it weren't her business to know. So guess what Maybelle done? She bought three grave spots at the highest point in the cemetery, the ones them same church folks said was closest to heaven, so they cost more. Then, Maybelle got herself this legal paper gived her permission to move MeeMaw and me on up there to wait on Mama. So, they dugged us up! Ain't that something? Took what they thought was us and carried our casket beds on up the hill. They was bringing Mama up in the hearse Maybelle hired, once the undertaker fella finished doing her hair. Lexie Ann sent Wanda on over to do it first, but Wanda cried so much, the funeral mens made her leave. Said they'd see to it theirselves. Lexie Ann had a fit.

"Nadine never wore her hair that way in her life!" she said.

"Now Lexie, honey, settle down," Melvin said. "Nadine don't care how it looks, by now. She's off yonder." Which probably weren't the truth. Mama always cared how her hair looked, but Lexie was close to having the new baby, and Melvin most likely wanted to calm her down. Probably said the first thing popped in his mouth. Mama's hair weren't too bad; I seen it look worse when Ray pulled a bunch of it out once. But Aunt Lexie carried on something awful. I think she was just griefed over everything that had happened and Mama's hair just gived her a way to scream it out, 'cause Mama's hair looked sorta okay, excepting where they bunched it back behind her ears real good. That made 'em stick out like that little Dopey fella in the *Snow White* book Alice liked so much, and Mama's ears *never* sticked out before. But the rest looked okay.

While Lexie was having herself a hissy fit over Mama's hair, calling them fellas down at the funeral home place, asking where in thunder they went to hairdresser school, Maybelle was tending to another surprise. She bought a grave marker for Mama and me, fit right over the top of the both of us! She had our names carved on it in pretty letters. Mama's side said NADINE HOWARD DODSON and give her birthday and her death day. Maybelle told them to be sure and leave off Pruitt, or she weren't paying for it. Guess she still couldn't find it in her heart to forgive Ray. My side of the marker said HERE LIES LORI JEAN DODSON. There was flowers carved on top, and right below my name, Maybelle had them put the day I was born and next to that, the day I died. It was the same day, just different years. But the best part was below them dates! It said: HEAVEN GOT ITSELF ANOTHER ANGEL TODAY. Wasn't that nice? Here Maybelle was mighty sick and there she was, seeing about us. There weren't no reason for her to get MeeMaw a new marker. She used the one Ray bought for MeeMaw when she died. These mens just lugged it up to its new resting spot. It weren't as fancy as the one Maybelle got for me and Mama. Still, it looked right nice next to ours. Maybelle paid for everything. And she paid for the biggest bouquet of flowers I ever seen. Had some more spread all around the marker, too. In truth, it was 'bout the prettiest grave spot in the whole place. Probably in the whole world. Near perfect, it was, 'cept I wished she would of paid to have Carolee dug up and moved over next to my spot. But I reckon Carolee's folks might not of let her, even if Maybelle'd thought of it. Mr. Thompson never got over Carolee dying like she did. He near drunk himself to death; cursed everything and everyone around him. Connie Dee got herself a baby 'fore she got herself a husband, and she run off. Mrs. Thompson, she stays pretty much by herself; keeps out of Mr. Thompson's way. Mostly, she tends to Carolee's grave spot and it's right pretty, so I guess it's best Carolee stay there, where her mama takes herself a lot of comfort every morning when the sun comes up.

Poor Maybelle, she keeps getting sicker. I best pray for her real good. Seems only right, after all them nice things she done. Yep, I best pray it ain't her time yet, and that she gets herself well, 'cause she ain't really a bad person trying to get good; she's just a sick person trying to be well. It's true, she weren't always nice to people, but everybody's got some bad parts in 'em, mixed up with the good, don't they? Even Carolee, she was about the bestest person I knowed in the whole world, and she had herself a bad part. She liked to make faces at Darla Faye when she weren't looking and she stuck gum in Darla's hair once, on purpose even. Made her cry and Carolee laughed. That weren't nice. See what I mean?

So I hope Maybelle gets well. It'd make her real happy. Truth be known, it'd make me happy, too. I don't much wanna run into her up here, 'least not right off, anyway. I don't got a heavy heart against her or nothing. Look at all she done for us. I'd just like to have a little time to myself 'fore I run into her again, is all. And—if Mama gets to come—I reckon she won't want to see Maybelle first thing, neither.

Speaking on Mama, they never did find out who put that rat poison in her 'taters. They questioned a whole lotta people, too. I'd like to think it was someone who loved her, but it coulda been someone that didn't. I could find out for myself if I stayed a bit longer, but it's my time to move on.

Just think—I'm gonna see MeeMaw. Won't that be something? And Carolee; she'll be right surprised to see me comin' up yonder. I hardly growed any! And little Iris Anne—I ain't never even seen her yet. Won't that be cute? A little baby girl angel. I probably might even get to see Jesus. Never know. I'd sure like to. I want to ask him if he's doing okay, on account of what them peoples did to him with those nails and stuff. And for sure I want to ask him if it'd be okay if Mama come here, even though she killed Ray dead. I want him to know her heart was in the right place that day she done it, but the screws in her head come loose and she couldn't help herself none. MeeMaw said he's a fella got a really big heart hisself, so he'll probably understand. And don't forget forgiveness; that's about his favorite thing, forgiveness.

Guess what? A real bright pretty light's coming my way. Reckon I best be going. One time I heard some folks say, *Heaven can wait*, but I don't see it that way. But then, I'm seeing a whole lotta things different now, with better eyes than the ones I had before.

MeeMaw was right fond of saying, "Lori Jean, git a move on, honey. You'll be late." It's so strange. I can hear her speaking them same words to me this very moment. I can! Fancy that.

epilogue

"Isn't she pretty, Melvin?"

"That she is, Lexie. Pretty as her namesake."

"Baby girl, you got your name from an angel."

"Mama?"

"What, sugar?"

"Is Lori Jean really a angel?"

"Alice, honey, she sure enough is."

"Is that why you named the baby for her?"

"I named the baby for her, so we'll always have a part a' her with us."

"What part's that, Ma?"

"The best part, Irl. The part that rests in our heart."

"I don't understan', Mama."

"See, sugar, every time we call the new baby's name, our heart will skip a beat . . . and in that tiny little moment it skips, we'll have our Lori Jean with us once again. Now, isn't that nice?

"Uh-huh."

"Melvin, honey?"

"What, sugarplum?"

"Ya' think Lori Jean knows we got a new baby named for her?"

"No way a knowing for a fact, Lexie, but I'd like to think she does. That'd be right nice, wouldn't it, darlin'?"

"Oh, Melvin . . ."

"Right nice . . . sugarplum . . . right nice indeed. . . ."